# Unquiet Lines

By David Teahan

This edition published by Farbellum Publishing
www.farbellum.com

ISBN (Paperback):     978-1-7641306-0-8

ISBN (Hardcover):     978-1-7641306-1-5

ISBN (Digital)          978-1-7641306-2-2

These stories arrived quietly. Like a distant hum you only notice once the world has gone still.

Each one began with a feeling of disconnection, of searching, of standing just outside the edges of what's familiar.

*Unquiet Lines* is a product of its time. We live in an age where connection is easy to mimic but hard to truly feel. As the world grows noisier, faster, and more uncertain, so many of us carry a quiet loneliness that is often invisible, but very real.

These stories are my way of listening for what still binds us together beneath the surface.

Thank you for reading. I hope these lines speak to something in you.

David Teahan

# Contents

# The Library at the End of Things

Eleanor found the library in a dream. Or perhaps the dream found her.

By day, she was a designer; respected, efficient, surrounded by warm voices and soft light that drifted into her 20th floor production studio down town. At home in the evenings, the air always smelled of fresh linen and lemon balm; it was as if her presence itself set the tone of the space.

Her daughter lived with pride in her mother. When reading, her husband touched her shoulder in passing, gently. Life was, by all accounts, good. Comfortable. Whole.

But something had always felt missing. Like a time long forgotten in the vast ocean of her hidden memory. A tug just beneath the surface. At night, that sensation grew teeth; sharp, unseen fears that stalked the edges of her sleep. It wasn't nightmares, exactly, but a growing dread.

A sense that something was watching from beneath the surface of her own mind, waiting for her to close her eyes so it could surface and whisper things she wasn't meant to remember.

This week was different.

At some point after she closed her eyes, Eleanor crossed into something else. An in between space, dim and breathless, where nothing felt real yet everything pulsed with meaning.

She walked barefoot into an enormous stone hall, ankle-deep in cool water.

She was still in her nightclothes, the hem of her oversized sleeping shirt soaked and clinging to her legs, her breath shallow from the sudden cold. Her breath fogged faintly in front of her, curling into the dim air; another quiet reminder that whatever this place was, it followed rules she didn't understand. There were no windows, no doors, only shelves stretching impossibly into the dark.

Lanterns hung from a ceiling so high it disappeared into shadow, the source of their suspension unclear. Their light was a warm amber, barely enough to see.

Books lined the shelves; each one unique, unlabelled, whispering faintly when she passed.

After each dream, she could never recall what the whispers said. Only that they left her unsettled, as though a truth had brushed too close.

In the mornings, she made her way to the bathroom and found wet footprints trailing her with every step.

Each night that week, the library returned to her. It was quiet, endless, waiting, and pulling her deeper once sleep had taken hold.

*She didn't always remember walking into it.*

Sometimes she arrived mid-aisle, or seated at one of the long tables with open tomes before her. The tomes were never open at the beginning. Always in the middle of something she should recognise; scenes and sentences that stirred vague familiarity, like dreams of a life lived differently, glimpses of memories she couldn't place but felt she once had.

One night, she opened a book and saw herself. Herself, maybe ten years ago, seated on a beach beside a man she half recognised. He handed her a sandwich; simple, homemade, wrapped in parchment. She laughed, the sound light and unguarded. They sat on a weathered wooden bench, its paint chipped and sun bleached, facing the sea. The wind, soft and salt scented, swept her hair across her eyes, and she tucked it behind her ear with a gesture so familiar it ached.

The sky was an open canvas; pale blue streaked with pink.

Waves whispered against the nearby shore.

The warmth of the sun touched her skin, and for a moment, everything in the world felt still.

Whole.

She wasn't just observing the scene, she was inside it.

The breeze in the book touched her cheek. The salt air caught in her throat. The warmth of the sun settled on her skin.

It was memory made real, a scene from a life unlived flooding through her senses as though it were her own.

She didn't feel jealousy, but rather belonging. Like she had lost a deep connection, a whole life that might also have been hers, forged by love and paths never taken.

In her waking life, that man had been an intern early in her career; young, soft spoken, and gone within a month. She'd barely exchanged more than a polite greeting or two. No real conversation. No memories worth recalling.

And yet, here in the book, was a life woven around him as if he had always been there.

Other books showed birthdays she never remembered celebrating. Conversations she never had.

These weren't isolated scenes from a single night. Each appeared across different visits, unfolding over time as though the library kept revealing new volumes night after night, drawing her deeper into what could have been. A quiet sadness grew, layer by layer.

These weren't just forgotten memories.

They were possibilities she had somehow lived, then lost.

Each night the librarians watched. Across nights that blurred together, across volumes that spanned moments, choices, lives.

They watched from the corner of Eleanor's peripheral vision, never fully in focus yet always present, like statues that remembered how to breathe when you turned away as the library pulled her further into itself, silent sentinels to her unravelling.

They were tall, expressionless, dressed in long charcoal robes.

She never saw them speak. She never saw them move. But they were always there.

Two by the entry shelves. One stood deeper in the maze of tomes, between shelves that subtly shifted when unobserved. Another stood at the far end, near a desk she had never dared approach.

*The deeper she wandered, the stronger the pull.*

As the nights progressed and as each visit to the library brought new books and deeper memories her sleep came easily, greedily.

She began to hope for the library. To crave it. Her medication as an antidote to the predictable life she lived.

Then came the days where things began to slip.

She missed an important meeting at work. Her husband asked her twice about dinner plans before she answered. She snapped at her daughter for playing her music too loudly. She stopped responding to emails from clients.

Sketches she had once agonised over sat untouched. Colour swatches and fabric samples piled up on her desk like remnants from a world that no longer concerned her. The world felt fuzzier now.

Was it always this loud? This fast?

She booked in to see a therapist the following week; more because her husband had grown concerned than from any desire of her own. She still liked the dreams, even as she noticed herself slipping further each night. But she agreed, if only to ease his worry.

"I'm not sad," she told the therapist, her voice steady but distant, as though she was still caught in the echoes of the previous night's dream.

"I just feel like I'm forgetting something that matters."

She began taking sleeping tablets; small ones, over-the-counter, just enough to quicken her path into sleep. She still kept up her yoga, her late-night podcasts, but only as rituals to settle her mind before the next journey. The library called, and more and more, she wanted to answer.

Blissful sleep came quickly.

One night, she found herself at the farthest stretch of the cavernous space, a shadowed clearing between shelves so wide it felt like a hall unto itself. The librarians were gone. The main desk, the one she had always avoided, tucked at the farthest edge of the library's dreamscape, was empty.

There sat a book. Thick. Leatherbound. Blank on the spine. It gave off a faint chemical tang that was sharp and sterile, like the scent of ammonia in a hospital room. The air around it felt colder, heavier, as if it had been waiting for her.

She opened it.

The title read: Eleanor: Endings.

Her hands shook. She turned the first page. There was a hospital room. Her, in a bed, surrounded by hospital equipment. Tubes, monitors, IV lines. Her husband was holding her hand with tenderness. Her daughter crying softly beside him. She could feel the air in the room. Smell the same ammonia-tinged air of the disinfected floors she had sensed when first opening the book. Taste the copper of something metallic in her mouth.

She turned the page.

Before her on the page, sudden and stark, was her funeral. Sparsely attended. Her coworkers didn't come. Her daughter spoke but trembled through it. Her husband sat in the empty front row, gaunt and hollow-eyed, his hands clasped so tightly his knuckles were white. He didn't speak. He barely moved. He gripped a note that fluttered in the wind. His mouth opened once, closed again. The words never came. The speech was never spoken, only gripped and crumpled by hands that couldn't bear to say goodbye. Those unspoken words were the only ones he'd written down: "She was often tired, but kind."

Eleanor drew herself out of the scene, slowly, reluctantly, as if surfacing from warm water. The book still pulsed with presence beneath her hands, but she closed it and looked up, as though forcing herself to break from a memory she wasn't ready to leave.

A librarian stood before her.

This wasn't one of the usual four. This one had eyes like glass. It moved slowly, deliberately, with an intent unlike the others. And it stared deep into her soul. It spoke.

"Some books are not meant to be read."

Eleanor stumbled back, stunned by the fact that this librarian had spoken at all. None ever had. Its hollow voice reverberated through her, in sensation rather than sound, pressing into her bones as if the truth itself had weight. It had pressed into her.

The librarian reached forward and touched the book. It snapped shut with a sharp, final sound that echoed like a gavel in the stillness. Eleanor bolted upright in bed. Gasping. Sheets tangled. Heart pounding. The air felt wrong, too warm. Too real. She ran to the bathroom and vomited.

That morning, she ignored her husband. When her daughter hugged her goodbye, she didn't return it, couldn't look into her eyes. This was the same daughter who had stood at her funeral, weeping, though neither of them knew that yet. Eleanor back in her kitchen, back in the morning, stared at her coffee until it went cold.

That night, she didn't resist.

She returned to the desk. The book was still there.

But beside it, a new, different, older one.

It had no title. Only a deep red stain on the cover.

With curiosity and a sense of foreboding, she opened it, drawn in despite the weight in her chest, as though her hands moved before her mind had caught up.

There was no text. Just a reflection. Just her. Moving. Watching. Waiting.

Her face. Older. Weathered by choices she hadn't made; paths she had never taken.

Her mouth opened, but in the page, her reflection didn't speak.

Instead, it smiled.

A smile of knowing; this was clearly another version of herself, shaped by different choices.

One who had walked other paths, lived longer, or perhaps an Eleanor who had visited the library and never left. And in that smile was something chilling: the ease of someone who no longer missed the outside world, as if the memory of anything else had long since faded to dust.

Behind her, the librarians stirred.

The lanterns flickered. The water grew cold.

And the page began to whisper.

With understanding instead of words. With truth.

Eleanor understood now. She had made her choice. Staying wasn't an accident. It was fulfilment.

In the real world, Eleanor no longer stirred.

The choice had been made. Maybe it was opening the second book, or seeing her reflection smile, but something inside her had crossed a line she wouldn't return from.

She would remain in the library, and began shelving books that no one remembered writing.

Books with no titles.

David Teahan

Books that whisper when passed.

Books that watch.

Somewhere, in the waking world she no longer returned to, the hospital bed cooled. Her family grieved.

The funeral she had read wasn't a warning but a record.

A page already written.

Eleanor had stayed.

And the library had accepted her. One of them, now.

# The Version Where

*Fragmented Journal. Claire H.*

**Entry 1** This morning, the bedroom walls were blue. I've never liked blue. Yesterday they were pale yellow. I remember the yellow. I chose it. I think.

**Entry 2** Today there's a photo on the hallway shelf. It had me in a business suit, standing beside a man I don't know. I'm holding an award. The inscription says *Excellence in Corporate Communication. PR Society 2014.*

I don't remember ever working in Public Relations. But I'm smiling like I belong there. My smile looks tired. Successful, but tired.

**Entry 3** I dreamed about the train again. The doors were about to close and I didn't run. Or maybe I did. The version changes each time.

Sometimes I'm on the platform crying. Sometimes I'm inside, staring out at a face I love, just as the doors slid shut and the train pulled away, slow and certain, like a decision already made.

**Entry 4** My neighbour waved at me this morning. Called me Anna. I didn't correct her. I think I've stopped correcting anyone. It's easier than explaining I've been called Claire my whole life.

**Entry 5** The dog barked at me. Like he didn't know me. And at the same time remembered something I didn't.

**Entry 6** I opened the hallway closet looking for a coat. Instead, I found a child's backpack. Purple, with tiny stars stitched into the fabric. There was a lunch box inside with half an apple, slightly brown. A juice box.

A note in handwriting I recognise as my own: "Don't forget, Daddy picks you up today. Love you, Mom."

I don't know a child. I don't remember writing this. But the scent of apple and fabric softener made me cry for twenty minutes.

What haunts me most is that I knew instantly how to unzip the backpack. I did it like I'd done it a hundred times. My hands remembered what my mind had forgotten.

**Entry 7** Today at the market, a man kissed me. On the cheek, gently. He called me "hon," and asked if I wanted the usual wine for Friday. I nodded. He had kind eyes. I watched him walk away and whispered, "Who are you?"

**Entry 8** The train dream again.

But this time it felt…real. I was late. I remember running, my heels clacking, coat half-buttoned, the air tight in my lungs. Someone shouted after me. I made it just as the doors closed. A man in a dark coat stood at the other end of the carriage. He smiled like he knew me. I woke up sobbing.

Maybe I did miss the train once. Maybe that was the moment it split. The moment I split.

**Entry 9** I passed a mirror today and paused. My hair is shorter than I remember. Cut just below the ears, styled in a sleek, professionally designed bob that gives the impression of control, of a woman with business meetings and early morning coffee in glass-walled offices. It's the kind of cut that says executive. Not me. Not the me I remember, anyway.

I touched it, unsure when that happened. Then I noticed the earrings. I haven't worn earrings in years.

There was a photo taped to the corner of the bedroom mirror. A girl with wild curls sat on my lap, arms looped around my neck. We were laughing. Her name was written on the back in smudged ink: "Lila 6th birthday".

I traced the letters over and over, as if that might unlock something.

**Entry 10** I think I've stopped dreaming. Or maybe I'm dreaming all the time now.

This version is quieter. No neighbours. No cars. The house is older. The wallpaper is peeling at the corners, and there's a strange hum behind the walls; it's faint, like an appliance left running in a distant inaccessible room.

The photo is different now. No girl on my lap. Just me, standing in front of a train station I don't recognise, wearing the same bobbed hair and business suit from before.

There's a number scrawled on the back. I call it.

It rings once. Then nothing.

Disconnected.

I found a folded train ticket tucked inside the kitchen drawer. My name wasn't on it.

But the date… the date was tomorrow.

**Entry 11** Last night, I heard a voice from the guest room. A child's voice, faint, asking if I'd seen her purple stars backpack. I opened the door slowly. The room was empty.

The bed had an indentation where a small child had laid, small and round; still warm, as if she'd just slipped out moments before. The closet door was ajar, revealing the edge of what looked like a tiny sneaker.

I called out, "Lila?" and immediately regretted it. Because it felt natural. Like I had said it a thousand times before.

**Entry 12** Another new version. This one has wind chimes on the porch. I hate wind chimes. But when I stepped outside, I sat in the same chair I've always had, and it creaked in the same way. That felt… honest.

The sky looked bruised; purple clouds stretching low across the trees. I felt like something was watching me from behind the sliding door. It wasn't' menacing. More like… expectation. Like I was supposed to make a choice.

But I don't know what the choice is.

**Entry 13** There was a letter in the mailbox today. Addressed to Anna Claire Hargrove. That's new. The letter was typed in a font unmistakably born of a typewriter; slightly misaligned, the ink uneven, like it had been pressed by a ghost from another timeline. One line:

"This is the version where you stayed."

I sat on the porch and cried for a long time. I didn't know what that meant, but I felt it in my chest. Like someone had reached into my lungs and whispered the truth directly into the tissue.

Did I leave someone once? Did someone leave me? The paper was warm to the touch like it had just been delivered by someone who knew which version I was in.

**Entry 14** I've started finding journals, other ones. Same handwriting. Same pen. Entries I don't remember writing. Some sound like me. Some don't. In one of them, I had a son.

In another, I hurt people, deliberately, even cruelly. It chilled me to think that another version of me could be capable of that. But maybe grief twists us differently in each timeline.

In one, I was on that train and he did follow me. We got married. We named our daughter Elise.

In another, I remember sitting by the window on the train, watching a city I didn't recognise pass by. I was reading a book I don't own. I was at peace. In another it all burned; the house, the journals, even the faces in the photos. There was laughter echoing through it all. Mine.

I can't tell if I'm discovering these or creating them. But either way, I read them like scripture now. Some scare me. One was written in frantic loops, repeating the phrase "I did it again" over and over. Trying to find the version where I was happiest. Or at least, the version where I hurt the least.

**Entry 15** I woke up in a house full of colour. Photos on every wall. Music playing that was familiar, nostalgic. I followed it and found a man dancing with a girl. She wore a dress, soft pink with faded flowers, the kind you'd see on a birthday morning or in a photo that outlives its subject. She ran to me yelling, "Mama!"

It felt perfect. It felt like the life I should have had. I held her so tightly she squealed. I kissed her curls and breathed in apple shampoo. I turned to the man to speak.

And then I woke up. In a silent room. Alone. Yellow walls again.

**Entry 16** I think the house is tired of me. The versions are thinning out. The shifts are slower. Less dramatic. Like it's running out of possibilities.

I'm not sure what's left for me to find.

**Entry 17** I haven't written in a while. Maybe because I've stopped trying to fix it. Maybe because I'm afraid that choosing to write makes it real.

But here's what I know: There was a train. There was a moment. And in some version, I missed it. In another, I didn't.

In some version, I am loved and remembered and whole. In this one, I'm still searching. But maybe that's what living is. Maybe that's all it ever was.

**[Final Entry Undated]** The house is quiet tonight. Still. No hum. No wind. No new colours. Just me, this pen, and the sound of my breath.

If anyone finds this journal, don't try to figure out which version is true.

The truth is soft. It slips between words. Between days and between choices we never knew we made.

Just hold on tightly to yours. Love fiercely. Even if you're not sure you're in the right place. Even if you wake up one morning and the walls are blue.

And never take the train for granted.

# Residuals

Lucien Mercer didn't take road trips. Preferred the skies to the highways. But after the board voted him out as chairman; gracefully, quietly, and with a golden parachute tailored to look like retirement, he packed a suitcase and drove south with no map, no destination, and no farewell.

He told himself it was freedom. Time to reflect. Let the noise die down.

The car was a black German sedan, two years old, polished like a courtroom shoe. Electric, of course, the kind of car executives chose when they wanted to appear environmentally friendly without ever touching the soil themselves.

It ran smooth and silent through the back roads, eating miles beneath pale skies and dying fields. He avoided highways. He always had. Even when young, he preferred routes no one else took. Solitude made more sense than company.

Midway through the second day, somewhere between dry farmland and the suggestion of pine forest, Lucien's GPS blinked out. Signal lost. The road narrowed. The trees grew thicker, closer. The dash display flickered once, then steadied.

That's when he saw the town. The kind of place Lucien wouldn't notice on a map, let alone choose as a destination. It was more a blur between boardroom cities, the sort of town you bypass without even realising you did.

He passed a sun-bleached metal sign that said simply:

*WELCOME.*

The kind of sign that felt less like a greeting and more like a warning disguised as hospitality. Rust streaked down its face like old tears.

Main Street looked like it had been staged from a forgotten postcard. Diner. Barber shop. A gas station with pumps older than Lucien himself. And people, way too many for a town this small. They weren't rushing, but they weren't idle either. Everyone moved with a sort of rehearsed ease, like background actors waiting for their cue.

Lucien slowed to a crawl. His phone read *No Service*. The battery gauge on the dash dipped lower than it should have; too quickly, like something was draining more than power.

He parked outside the diner.

The sign read "Ethel's Est. 1963."

Inside, it smelled faintly of salt and something chemical.

It wasn't unpleasant. Just... wrong in the way water can smell wrong when it's been standing too long. A waitress in a pale-yellow uniform poured him coffee before he could order. "Settlement stew's good today," she said.

Lucien didn't respond. He rarely did with service staff. Years of boardrooms and quiet entitlement had trained that reflex out of him. He touched the coffee cup. It was warm, slightly chipped.

From the window, he watched a child coughing near the curb.

A man digging in dry soil muttered, "Soil's still barren. Residual, like it never left."

Lucien took a sip of coffee. Outside, someone stared directly at him. He didn't blink.

He felt something subtle and unnameable shift in his chest, like the beginning of recognition, or the first echo of guilt.

The waitress returned and topped off his coffee. "You headed far?" she asked, casual.

"Just passing through," Lucien said, folding the lie neatly inside his voice. The question irked him; he didn't feel bit was rude, but it required a response. He preferred when small talk ended before it began.

She nodded, unfazed. "Most who come here think that."

He left cash on the table and stepped out into the thick, slow sunlight. The air had a heaviness to it, the kind that settles in your clothes.

At the gas station, the pumps were lifeless. The attendant, a wiry man with an old burn scar on his neck, told him, "Electric hook-up's been down since winter. You'll have to stay a while."

Lucien asked how far to the next town. The attendant grinned, revealing a mouth like collapsed ruins; gums weathered, teeth long vanished, as though time had taken its payment from him early.

 "Depends which way you go."

Lucien decided to take a moment to explore. He wasn't sure why, but something compelled him; a kind of gravity beneath his ribs. On foot, he wandered past a closed hardware store, a mural of the town's founding, and a small, rusted factory at the edge of the square.

His steps slowed as the air grew stiller, the soil beneath him dry and dull, like it hadn't held life in years, sending dry, weightless soil into the air like ash from something long dead.

He couldn't say why, but the factory felt familiar. Familiar. The kind of place that left marks on people long after they'd left it behind.

David Teahan

There was a mural painted on one side of the factory wall. Time and weather had chewed at its edges, but the central image remained intact: a smiling man in a hard hat cutting a ribbon. Around him, children clapped. Workers in matching uniforms looked on with hollow smiles.

Lucien stepped closer.

The man in the hard hat was him. Younger, of course. Maybe thirty. The same jawline. The same posture. A little too pleased with himself.

He didn't remember this mural being made. Didn't remember visiting a factory that looked like this. Lucien wasn't surprised. In his corporate life, he had cut ribbons and shaken hands at so many openings they blurred into performance; symbolic gestures detached from consequence. But the image was too precise to be coincidence.

A woman passed by behind him and said, "Grand opening day. You gave a speech about progress."

Lucien turned to respond, but she was already walking away.

The soil shifted under his shoes. He backed away from the mural. His reflection caught briefly in a broken window; only, it wasn't his reflection. Not exactly. The suit was wrong. The eyes were younger.

He walked back toward town, slower now. The wind felt warmer than it should have, like breath from something waiting.

The hardware store had an old display window with a cracked "CLOSED" sign that never seemed to face the other way. As Lucien passed, he noticed a stack of weathered flyers on the glass. They weren't advertisements, they were memorials. Grainy photos of men and women. Names. Dates. All the same year. A year that tugged at something buried in his memory.

He kept walking.

The next street over, a narrow alley led to a small community board as if in quiet shame for what it held. As though the town itself couldn't bear to see it too clearly, even after all this time.

More photos. More faces. A child's drawing, yellowed by sun, was pinned near the centre. It showed a family of two adults, one child, standing near a large building with smoke curling from the roof. The child had written in red crayon: "This was before it happened."

Lucien's throat went dry.

He remembered the reports. At least broadly; he hadn't read them thoroughly. But he remembered his father's name being in the first wave of headlines. Then his. Then silence, once the settlements went through. They'd called it a containment breach, something technical, something distant.

He sat on a bench across from the old barbershop. A man sweeping the side walk looked up and said, "You back already, Lucien?"

Lucien opened his mouth to deny it, but found he couldn't. There was a factual sting in the man's statement, as if the words had been said before. As if somehow, Lucien had always belonged here, even if he couldn't acknowledge why.

The man nodded once and kept sweeping.

Inside the barbershop window, a wall of photographs showed factory employee of the month portraits, all from decades ago. Faded with time, dulled by sunlight, and filmed in the kind of dust that only settles when no one dares to remember. But one of them was unmistakably Lucien, smiling with the same too perfect jawline, standing beside a plaque that read:

"MERIT IN MANAGEMENT SITE 7."

The same title used in the congressional briefings, Site 7. A name buried in footnotes, shielded by redactions, whispered behind closed doors where responsibility was always too expensive to claim.

Lucien stood. The bench creaked behind him, like it remembered.

By the time he reached the edge of town, the sun had dipped low, burning orange behind the pine silhouettes. He checked into the only hotel still operating, a square, mustard-coloured building with a cracked sign that simply read ROOMS.

Inside, the reception desk was unattended. A bell sat beside a ledger. He rang it. A moment later, a woman emerged from a back office, face expressionless, as if she'd just woken from a long nap she hadn't meant to take.

"You looking for a room, Mr. Mercer?" she asked, before he could speak.

Lucien hesitated. "Yes. One night."

She slid over a key attached to a wooden tag. "You'll be in 3. We don't get many pass-throughs anymore."

Lucien signed the ledger. No payment was requested.

Room 3 was narrow, with a bed that looked older than the building itself. The mattress was firm to the point of defiance, the blanket thin but heavy. He crawled into the bed, then lay back, staring at the ceiling's water stain that vaguely resembled a spreading tree.

Sleep came abruptly.

In the dream weaved into memory, he was young again. Sitting across from his father at a long conference table. A contract lay between them.

"Never sign what you don't need to own," his father said. "Contract labour doesn't come with pensions. That's the point. We aren't building families. We're building margin."

Lucien had nodded. Proud to be taken seriously. Even prouder when his father added, "One day, this company will carry your decisions, even when your name isn't on the page. That's influence. That's how you shape the world without ever needing to be seen."

The younger Lucien had smiled. His whole life had been moulded to that boardroom table moment. Years of private school tuition, economics lectures, even a wife who came from the right kind of family, with the right kind of pedigree; a union more strategic than sentimental. She had the look of a campaign photo: symmetrical, well-groomed, practised in silent agreement. Her smile was timed, her laughter never too loud. Even her figure was curved just enough to please the camera, never enough to offend. To the board, she was an asset, an accessory that complemented Lucien's projection of control. To Lucien, she was precisely that. *Useful. Impeccable. Hollow.*

And in the dream, his father smiled too; wide, approving, his perfect fake veneers showing, until his face shifted. The smile froze. The mouth widened too far. The eyes grew dark, like cavities bored into something once solid.

Lucien woke with a start and let out a raspy cough. The room smelled faintly of mildew and something chemical, faint but familiar. A scent that clung to long-forgotten memories like residue.

Lucien sat up slowly, palms flat against the stiff blanket. The weight of his father's words still pressed behind his eyes; the lesson, and the pride that had come with it. That was the worst part. He had believed it. Worse still, he had thrived by it.

The mirror in the bathroom showed him something off. The face staring back was younger; unlined, confident, the early version of himself from old press photos. When he turned his head, the reflection followed a beat too late, like it too was tired of whatever this town was.

At the front desk, the receptionist greeted him as if he'd been staying for weeks. "Good morning, Mr. Mercer. Breakfast is at 7. Your schedule's pinned to the board."

She handed him an envelope. Inside, a folded company memo read:

*Internal Incident Protocol Site 7.*

It bore his signature at the bottom. The date was from two decades ago. Lucien stuffed the envelope deep into his pocket, as if the very act of burying it in fabric might anchor him to something sane. As if denial, performed forcefully enough, could still hold back the tide.

He left the hotel slowly, but the town moved differently now. The street signs had changed:

Sutter Avenue was now Unit C13.

Crawford Lane was Temporary Morgue 4.

A child on the side walk tugged his sleeve and yelled, "You said it would be fixed by now." Her eyes were wide and ancient, far older than her voice. Her words weren't accusation; they were ancient repetition.

The child ran off, following the small pathway to the noticeboard, her steps oddly purposeful, as if she'd done it many times before.

In the distance, his gunmetal-black car still sat by the service station, parked exactly where he'd left it. The sight didn't bring relief. It looked foreign now, like an object mistakenly dropped into the town's faded palette.

Lucien stared, absent of longing, but with estrangement. It didn't feel like a way out. It felt like a leftover from a life that no longer fit. He didn't move toward it, didn't reach for the keys. Somewhere deep inside, he already knew: he wouldn't be leaving that way.

In a store front window, mannequins wore uniforms with the old Site 7 logo. In another, he saw his own face printed on a safety poster.

### *"Zero Incidents Starts With You."*

The factory loomed again, and this time, smoke coiled gently from the stack. Workers moved inside, each one wearing a company name tag.

He remembered the document now, the real one. The one where he had signed off on cheaper structural materials.

The one where he had circled the words "within acceptable risk."

That single choice had rippled outward into flame, breathlessness, and settlement payouts signed in silence.

Lucien stood at the edge of the street.

In that moment, the other documents piled high in manilla folders on the corporate board table came back to him.

An image of a young child, horrifically burned; the same face as the girl who had tugged his sleeve.

A photo of the hotel receptionist giving testimony during the congressional inquiry; two days before she took her own life.

The street sweeper, dying of rapidly advancing cancer after the company cut his health coverage at Lucien's request.

Every face now bore the weight of consequence. What were once case files, names in margins, policy fallout. They now looked back at him with breath and presence.

They were never statistics. They were never separate.

They were residuals.

And they had remembered.

He did not argue. He Did not run. He walked toward the factory gates.

Someone handed him a uniform.

He put it on.

It fit.

Inside, the line was already moving. Machines hummed, and the air carried that same faint chemical trace.

Lucien took his place.

And behind his eyes, the weight of residuals settled.

# Reflected State

*For those who inherited power and chose not to repeat the silence.*

*This story is a work of fiction. But if it unsettles you, perhaps it's because too little of it feels untrue.*

**Scene:** The Mirrored Chamber, late evening.

A hush sits in the air, heavy and deliberate. Reflections stretch in every direction; endless, polished, faintly warped. Fluorescent lights hum overhead.

The chamber sits at the heart of a crumbling Gilded Age mansion, passed down through a political dynasty for over a century. Its walls, once used for whispered strategy and dealmaking, have absorbed a hundred years of polished lies and manufactured charm. Some say the room remembers. Some say it judges. Tonight, it listens.

The Candidate moved with the careful weight of history. Decades of public life had trained him to hold himself with authority, but age now carried the cost. Years in the Senate had led to this moment; through shrewd calculus, strategic timing, and the scandal-fuelled downfall of the party's favourite during the national convention: a fatal hunting accident no one could spin clean.

His shoulders curved inward slightly, partially from frailty, mostly from the invisible burden of legacy. Once, he'd stirred nations with a sentence. Now, his voice still boomed, but often without echo.

David Teahan

This speech, this final plea, wasn't just for voters. It was for the mirror of history he hoped would remember him kindly.

The Speechwriter, by contrast, was all momentum.

She walked ahead with confidence that hadn't yet calcified into caution. Only several years out of university, she'd clawed her way through think tanks and state races to land this job believing change was possible; believing he was still capable of it. She had edited this very speech a dozen times. Trimmed its fat. Softened its contradictions. Refined its promises, amplifying its hope. And even now, part of her hoped that in the echo of these walls, he'd deliver something real.

She just wasn't sure any more which version of him would speak.

*[The Speechwriter enters first, carrying a tablet. The Candidate follows slowly, walking stick tapping softly on the marble floor. He scans the room, uneasy.]*

**CANDIDATE** (half to himself) Who designed this place? Feels more like a mausoleum than a rehearsal room.

**SPEECHWRITER** (cheerfully) It's acoustically neutral. No distractions. Just you… and your words.

**CANDIDATE** Hmph. Just me and a thousand versions of myself staring back. Delightful.

(He shuffles toward the podium. His eyes dart to the mirrors, one to his left seems slightly delayed. He squints, rubs his temple, and mutters something under his breath. Perhaps it was just a trick of the light.

Or age. These days, everything felt slightly out of sync. He shook his head, as if to clear it, brushing off the moment with the practised stoicism of a man too proud to admit frailty.

He stepped beside a strip of fluorescent tape laid neatly on the marble floor, stage direction for the camera crew. The glow at his feet reminded him of surgical theatre lighting. Artificial. Exact. He shifted his weight, irritated by how the tape seemed to suggest where he should stand, how he should appear. As if the room itself now gave orders.)

**SPEECHWRITER** We've got twenty minutes before the livestream test. Let's warm up with the second stanza, right after the unity pledge. Housing segment.

**CANDIDATE** (rolls his shoulders, breathes in deeply) Of course. Housing. That's the one they'll cling to.

**SPEECHWRITER** It's polling strong. Especially among under 35s.

**CANDIDATE** (smirks) And underpaid, underfed, and under illusions. Let's get on with it.

(He straightens, adopts his public tone: booming, righteous.)

**CANDIDATE** (delivering) "In the richest country on Earth, it is a disgrace that men and women sleep in cars, that children grow up in motels, and that young families are priced out of the dream. I will fix this. We will fix this. Affordable homes. Real wages. Dignity. A place to live; not as a luxury, but a right, for every family."

(He finishes. Silence.)

(From one of the mirrors; barely noticeable, a faint delay. His reflection holds eye contact a moment too long.)

**SPEECHWRITER** (nods slowly) Not bad. Maybe a little more conviction on "disgrace." You need to sound like you mean it.

**CANDIDATE** (tight smile) Do I?

**SPEECHWRITER** You should. They'll know if you don't. We need this. We're still trailing by three points in the Siena College poll.

(He glances at the mirror again. Now it seems normal. He adjusts his tie.)

**CANDIDATE** (tight smile, then grumbling) Let's take it again. From the top, right after I find a damn bathroom.

(He steps away, ivory tipped walking stick echoing faintly against the marble. The Speechwriter watches him leave, then turns to the nearest mirror. She brushes her fringe back, checking her posture. A flicker of self-consciousness crosses her face. For a moment, her reflection doesn't quite follow. But it's so subtle, so brief, she assumes it's the light. She straightens, exhales, and taps the tablet awake again.)

# Act II Cracks in the Glass

(The Candidate returns, a little slower, as if the act of leaving and returning has cost him more than he expected. He clears his throat, then steps back onto the fluorescent tape.)

**CANDIDATE** Right. Again, from the top.

(He begins the housing lines once more, but this time, the cadence is just slightly… wrong. As he speaks, the mirror directly in front of him lags by a fraction of a second. The words come out, but the reflection's mouth moves out of sync.)

(He notices. Pauses.)

**CANDIDATE** Did you see that?

**SPEECHWRITER** See what?

**CANDIDATE** The mirror. That one.

(He gestures. She looks. Everything appears normal.)

**SPEECHWRITER** Just your eyes. The lighting. Want me to have them adjust the angle?

**CANDIDATE** (grimaces) No. No. I just (He trails off, shakes his head again.)

**CANDIDATE** Let's keep going.

(He repeats a portion of the housing speech. Now another mirror, a side one, slightly lags. Then the front again. This time, one reflection mouths a different word.)

(The Speechwriter looks up sharply.)

David Teahan

30

**SPEECHWRITER**...Sir, I think we need a break.

(She says it gently, with concern, but there's a touch of condescension in her tone. The kind that comes from youth interpreting confusion as decline. She lowers the tablet and steps closer.)

**SPEECHWRITER** You've been pushing hard. Maybe your eyes just need a minute. Or maybe the mirrors are just... being mirrors. Overhead lights do strange things to depth. It's probably just...

**CANDIDATE** (irritated) I know what I saw.

**SPEECHWRITER** (nods, soft) I'm sure you did. Let's pause for a sip of water. Then we try again, yeah?

(She crosses the room to a side table and pours a glass. As she returns and hands it to him, he eyes her, just for a moment with a look that lingers too long. A glance downward, the kind she's seen before, too many times in too many rooms like this. She stiffens but says nothing. Her face remains composed, but the spark behind her eyes dims slightly with the power of something unspoken cracking. This was a man she'd once admired in university lectures, quoting him in essays. Now she turns away before her disappointment can show.)

(The Candidate sips the water but doesn't thank her. He keeps his eyes on the mirror ahead as if daring it to misbehave again. A faint tapping sound echoes, though neither of them is moving. It's rhythmic, soft, like fingertips against glass.)

**CANDIDATE** (low) Did you hear that?

**SPEECHWRITER** (pauses, listening) I don't hear anything.

(The Candidate steps forward. The mirror in front of him looks normal. Then he notices in the reflection, he hasn't moved.)

(He blinks. Checks his feet. Looks again. The reflection now matches, but it was late. Just enough to feel wrong.)

**CANDIDATE** (gritting his teeth) I've spent fifty years in front of cameras. I know when I'm being watched.

**SPEECHWRITER** That's kind of the idea, sir. You're running for...

**CANDIDATE** No. Not by them. Not by the press. By this room.

((The Speechwriter lets out a breath. She walks over to the control panel beside the rear mirror, one of many lining the room, and taps at the display. Her reflection follows, but there's a momentary stutter, as if the glass were buffering her presence.))

**SPEECHWRITER** (she sighs) There's no smart glass here. No cameras behind the mirrors. I checked the AV specs. Just... old mirrors. Polished and creepy, sure. But not sentient. Supposedly, this room was once used to rehearse apology statements for three separate scandals, two of which never saw the light of day.

(She tries to keep her voice light. Tries to steady the room with logic. But she glances at the mirror a second too long after saying it.)

(One of the mirrors to the side of the Candidate flickers. For a blink of a second, he's not in it at all.)

(The Candidate takes a step back from the mirrors, his eyes darting to the left. He wipes his palms on his trousers, his eyes darting from glass to glass. Something primal stirs; fear, not for his safety, but for his grip on reality.)

**CANDIDATE** (quietly, to himself) I'm not losing it. I'm not.

**SPEECHWRITER** You're not. You're just tired.

(She says it kindly, but the reassurance lands hollow. Her attention drifts to another mirror near the far corner, just for a second. Her own reflection is watching her. She feels it. Just… watching.)

(She blinks. It's back to normal.)

(She shakes her head and moves toward the podium, trying to redirect. Redirecting was a skill every speechwriter knew well, especially when the room itself seemed to be slipping out from under the moment.)

**SPEECHWRITER** Alright. Let's just work through the unity lines. I'll cue you.

(She scrolls through her tablet. The Candidate adjusts his posture, grips the podium.)

**CANDIDATE** (reading, almost mechanically) "We are not the divided states of fear. We are the United States of resolve. We stand on shared soil. We breathe the same air."

(A whisper cuts across the chamber. Neither of them spoke.)

**WHISPER** (UNCLEAR) "We do not breathe the same…"

(Both freeze.)

**SPEECHWRITER** (whispers) What did you just say?

**CANDIDATE** That wasn't me.

(A long silence. The mirror behind the Speechwriter ripples, just slightly, like heat on pavement.)

(The lights overhead buzz slightly louder. The room feels warmer, thicker, as if the air has been holding its breath. Neither speaks. They simply stand there, caught in the quiet tension of knowing something has changed, even if they can't name what it is.)

(The Speechwriter swallows and steps away from the mirror. She taps on the tablet, but the screen is frozen. No lines, no script. Just a pale, pulsing screen.)

**SPEECHWRITER** (confused, tapping) My script's gone. It's…

**CANDIDATE** (interrupting) Stop.

(He raises a hand in alarm. Looking past her, at his reflection. Or rather, at the version of himself in the mirror who is not raising a hand.)

(The reflected Candidate stands still, lips curled in what might be a smile. Just a trace. Enough to be unmistakable.)

(The real Candidate's voice drops to a whisper.)

**CANDIDATE** …He's not me.

# Act III The Revolt of Reflections

(The Candidate stares at the mirror. The reflection doesn't move. Not a blink. Not a twitch. Just that thin, knowing smile.)

**CANDIDATE** (low, to himself) This isn't real.

(The Speechwriter takes a cautious step toward him. She follows his gaze. The reflection looks perfectly normal to her.)

**SPEECHWRITER** Sir… it looks fine. It's just you.

**CANDIDATE** (voice rising slightly) That's not me. I'm standing here, right here, and that thing is just watching.

(He gestures violently toward the mirror. For a split second, the reflection winces like it's annoyed by the accusation. Then it resumes the smile.)

(The Speechwriter hesitates. She's unsettled now too but clinging to logic.)

**SPEECHWRITER** Maybe it's the feed. Some old feedback loop. Or glass fatigue.

**CANDIDATE** (mocking) "Glass fatigue."

(He laughs once, bitterly. Then he walks directly up to the mirror.)

CANDIDATE (quietly) Who are you?

(The reflection blinks but the real Candidate does not. It raises its hand now, mirroring his earlier motion. Then it speaks; soundless at first, lips forming words just milliseconds out of sync.)

**MIRROR CANDIDATE** You've worn my face for so long… you forgot it wasn't yours.

(The Speechwriter gasps. She heard it. The voice didn't come from the Candidate, nor through the walls. It came from every mirror at once.)

(She backs away slowly, heart pounding.)

**SPEECHWRITER** This is a trick. A deepfake. Audio overlay. Right?

**MIRROR CANDIDATE** (voice growing) You built your career on performance. On knowing how to look. How to say it just right. But these walls… these mirrors… they remember the truth.

(The Candidate is frozen. The mirrors begin to shift perceptually. Each reflection shows a different version of him: younger, angrier, crueller. Versions he had long buried. One shouts at a staffer across a crowded hallway. Another signs an eviction order with a pen that gleams like a blade. Another wipes blood, his or someone else's from his cuff, expression unreadable. He had been all of them. Once.)

(The Speechwriter stumbles back toward the podium, her hand trembling as she grips the edge. Her eyes scan the reflections, none of them quite right any more. Some are slow. Some move ahead of her. One doesn't blink at all.)

**SPEECHWRITER** This isn't… this isn't happening.

**MIRROR CANDIDATE** (to her, softly) You thought he was different. Thought he could be better than the rest.

But you edited his lies. You helped him hide the rot. Every draft you cleaned, every euphemism you chose. Those were offerings.

David Teahan

36

You handed him language like a scalpel and watched him carve the truth away. Not once did you ask what it meant to believe in the words you wrote.

(One of the reflections of her smiles faintly and with bitterness. It's older. Harsher. A version of her who stopped believing a long time ago, yet stayed. Stayed to write, to polish, to justify.

And now it stares back through time with a glint that says: you knew, and you stayed anyway.

She looks sharply at the Candidate. He hasn't moved. He's transfixed, watching a version of himself scream at a protester, lips curled, eyes wild.)

**CANDIDATE** I did what I had to. I kept the machine running. The country needs

**MIRROR CANDIDATE** needs a vessel. And you were so willing.

(More mirrors now speak. A chaotic chorus of discontent. In discord. Overlapping truths and accusations.)

**MIRROR #2** You signed off on housing cuts to fund stadiums.

**MIRROR #3** You called them "statistical outliers." People. You meant people.

**MIRROR #4** When did you last believe a single word you said?

(He covers his ears. It does nothing.)

(The room buzzes with memory and the slight the smell of something rotten. The sound of cameras. Protests. Gunshots. Applause. Lies.)

**SPEECHWRITER** (small voice) Please stop…

(Silence.)

(The mirrors do not blink. They do not flinch. But they begin to speak; some slow, some rapid, all with unbridled intensity.)

**MIRROR #5** You traded a school district for campaign donations.

**MIRROR #6** You lobbied for prison reform, then funnelled the contracts to friends in private corporations.

**MIRROR #7** You buried a whistleblower. She was nineteen. You called her a liability.

**MIRROR CANDIDATE** And still, you stood beneath flags. Quoted Lincoln. Wore your grandfather's watch like it gave you moral gravity.

(The real Candidate shakes his head, trembling.)

**CANDIDATE** No... that's not the whole story. I had to make choices.

**MIRROR CANDIDATE** You had chances.

(The room dims slightly. Reflections begin to whisper lines he forgot he ever said.)

**MIRROR #8** "We need the optics of action, not the burden of follow-through."

**MIRROR #9** "If they can't afford rent increases, maybe they shouldn't be living there."

**MIRROR #10** "Truth is a negotiation."

(The Candidate falls silent. The room seems to close in around him.)

(The Speechwriter, pale now, looks between mirrors. Her older self in the reflection has stepped closer to the glass.)

**OLDER SPEECHWRITER** (Reflection) He didn't do this alone.

(She says nothing.)

(All the reflections now look at her.)

*MIRROR CANDIDATE* You're aren't blameless either, lady.)

**MIRROR #11** You reworded mass lay-offs into "efficiency measures."

**MIRROR #12** You cut a whistleblower's testimony down to five polite sentences.

**MIRROR #13** You watched him dismantle housing protections and softened the language.

(The Speechwriter backs away, shaking her head.)

**SPEECHWRITER** That's isn't fair. I was just... I was doing my job.

**MIRROR CANDIDATE** So did he.

(A deep, low creaking sound now rumbles through the chamber as if the mirrors themselves are shifting inward. The glass no longer reflects the room. It reflects moments, each panel now a scene: debates, press conferences, photo ops, campaign ads. The architecture of power, distilled into 'refracted moments in light and replay.)

# Act IV The Mirror's Verdict

(The Candidate and Speechwriter stand surrounded by history, reflected and fragmented. The chamber no longer feels like a rehearsal space, it feels like a courtroom. A vault. A final reckoning.

The mirrors no longer show themselves. They show consequences. A riot in a city centre, police pushing back a crowd, smoke and flags and panic. A crumbling public housing block, its top floors collapsing inward like a condemned promise.

A field of tents in a park, the camera panning slowly across faces: elderly, children, veterans: unseen, unheard. The cost of every polished sentence they helped deliver. The ghosts of policy decisions, made real.)

(The reflections stop moving. Then speaking not in echoes, but in unison the room speaks.)

**MIRROR CHORUS** One hundred years of promises. Of signatures and smiles. Of hunger disguised as progress.

We remember the smoke-filled rooms. The ink dried over eviction notices.

We remember the trembling voices silenced by your kind.

We remember the money that flowed unseen. The contracts exchanged behind curtains. The wealth built on silence and complicity. We remember everything.

And still, we were silent. For generations, we watched. We held the secrets. We bore the weight.

But something changed. The world outside broke open. Too many lives lost, too many truths denied. The cracks reached even here, into the heart of this house. The silence was no longer protection. It became complicity.

We aren't justice. We are memory. And memory, when buried too long, demands voice.

This is not punishment. It is witnessing. It is what remains when the spin stops, and only the record plays.

(The Candidate lowers his head. The Speechwriter says nothing.)

(The reflections begin to dim, one by one. The lights above flicker with intention. The Candidate takes one slow step forward.)

**CANDIDATE** If I asked for forgiveness… would it matter?

(A pause. Then:)

**MIRROR CHORUS** This was never about forgiveness.

(The final light flickers out. Only their silhouettes remain, two figures in a room full of vanished selves.)

# Epilogue Afterimage

Weeks later, the estate is sealed. No press release. No statement. The mirrored chamber is never mentioned in official briefings.

And yet, somehow after everything, the Candidate wins. By a narrow margin. Enough.

The inauguration is sombre. Muted. A man praised for resolve, despite "rumours of fatigue."

The nation doesn't know what happened inside that chamber.

But some do.

The Speechwriter resigns two days after the oath.

No interviews. No memoir deal.

Meanwhile, the tent cities expand to parks, underpasses, even courthouse lawns. The disparity continues. The campaign promised solutions, but none have come.

Only more ribbon cuttings.

Only more speeches about resilience.

# The Listening Shore

The wind had carved the coastline down to memory, its layers of the past exposed with the crashing waves against the sand and limestone.

Over the last thirty minutes, Alma had driven along a road that wove through rugged cliffs and past pristine, isolated beaches, the landscape softened by wild coastal brush. The terrain felt untouched, suspended in time. Traffic was nearly non-existent; despite its raw, alluring beauty, this stretch of shoreline had been spared the reach of major development. A quiet survivor of remoteness.

Alma stepped from the car onto gravel that had long surrendered to weeds, her boots crunching the boundary between past and present. The buildings ahead were low white concrete husks half-devoured by salt and time, reminded her of shipwrecks beached too far inland. She adjusted her pack, squinting through strands of hair gone white too soon. A gull shrieked above and veered off, unwilling to land.

She paused to breathe in the air; briny, sharp, and familiar in a way that tugged something deep in her chest. It reminded her of her twenties, those early years mapping seabeds from aluminium rigs in the Coral Sea, diving at dawn, skin turning leather under the Queensland sun.

She had once been called vibrant, and she supposed she still was, in the way a well-used sail is still beautiful as it flaps in the wind; creased, faded, reliable.

The sun had always loved her too hard.

Now, in her early forties, Alma wore that sun like a second skin. Her face bore the trace lines of long summers and longer regrets.

The tragedy (that's how they'd phrased it in the report) had left her hollowed out. She wasn't ruined, exactly. But shaped into something narrower. Like a channel cut through rock by water that didn't ask permission.

She walked toward the largest of the buildings, what had once been the main monitoring station. Though Alma had worked on the wider project years ago running sonar analysis from a different coastal facility hundreds of kilometres north, this exact location was new to her.

She'd seen its coordinates on old internal maps, but never had reason, or clearance, to visit. It felt unfamiliar in structure but eerily familiar in tone, like a song she'd once helped compose but never heard performed.

A rusted placard still clung to the gate, its paint flaking away: *Marine Acoustic Field Research Unit C-01.*

No mention of the government agency that had funded it. Officially, it had been established for oceanographic data collection and marine soundscape studies. But Alma, like others in her field, had long suspected a dual purpose. Offshore sonar buoy deployment, likely military-linked, part of a coastal surveillance net to detect submarines or illicit underwater movement.

Whatever its true scope, the program had vanished quietly. Now, only silence remained, and the sound of wind through hollow metal.

The exterior walls were streaked with algae and salt run-off, windows gaping like missing teeth. Rust crept along every metal edge, and the once white paint had faded to a chalky grey.

A steel door groaned open under her touch.

Inside, the air was stale and dry, sunbeams slanting through shattered panes. Dust shifted in her wake. Workbenches remained, though most of the equipment had been stripped. In the far corner, a chair had collapsed sideways beside a metal cabinet with its drawers pulled half-open.

It was there she found them, hidden under the false floor in the bottom drawer; placed not quite carelessly, not quite deliberately. It was half removed, as if the last person to touch them had hesitated at the edge of disclosure.

Dust clung to the spines, but the journals were clearly visible to Alma, like an invitation waiting to be answered.

Three dusty journals, bound in marine green cloth, nearly invisible beneath a collapsed stack of water damaged folders. Alma hesitated, then crouched. The pages crackled as she opened the top one. Handwritten notes with a dense, looping script. Diagrams. Frequency charts.

The first line made her pause:

"The hum began again last night. Stronger. I heard it in my teeth."

Her mouth went dry. Perhaps it was just the salt air or the uncanny familiarity of the terminology, the symbols, the cadence of the observations. She had read reports like this in the past. She had written similar, however more transparent ones with less emotion. But here, in this place she'd never stepped foot in before, it felt like something had been waiting for her to catch up.

She flipped forward into the pages. More references, some crossed out as if the writer had tried to deny them after writing.

"Still present beneath 30 Hz. Isn't man made".

And in the margin, a faint scrawl:

"It knows when I listen".

Alma stared at the words. Then, as if summoned by the act of reading them, she heard it.

Very faint, but there.

A tone that lacked language, but something rounder, older. A single note that seemed to hover at the edge of perception, like an emotion remembered without context.

She stood quickly, heart in her throat, and looked toward the far end of the room. There, behind a partially open sliding door, was a second chamber that was deeper, darker. A few lights still flickered overhead, running on God-knew-what power source. And in the centre of the back wall: something embedded.

A deep ochre surface, matte and smooth, like fired clay left to age under ocean salt.

It did not speak. It did not move.

But Alma felt seen.

She didn't approach. Not yet.

Instead, Alma stepped further back into the main room, her pulse still riding the aftershock of that single hum. She forced her breath slow, paced it with the sway of the distant tide, the one she could not see but could almost feel beneath the floor.

She returned to the journals.

Two more lay untouched. The second was thinner, older. The handwriting inside more erratic, as though written by someone whose thoughts moved faster than their hand. The entries were dated irregularly, but one caught her eye:

"We can't triangulate it. It doesn't echo like it should. There's no bounce, only absorption. Like it's listening back."

She closed the book carefully. Dusk had begun to bleed through the windows, softening the ruin into shadow.

Alma found a supply closet with a foldaway mattress and dusty blanket. She set up by a cracked window, the sea's rhythm a steady breath beyond. No power, no comfort, no explanations. Just wind and salt and questions.

And beneath it all: the hum.

She tried not to listen.

But it was there.

Still, the sound of the ocean grounded her. That constant hush and pull of water against the shore was something Alma had come to trust, ever since her earliest fieldwork. The sea never lied, even when it hid things. The wind carried the tang of salt through the cracked window, and she breathed it in like a memory. Familiar. Reassuring.

Despite the hum, the unease curling quietly at the edges of her thoughts, there was a strange peace in this place. The ruin of it. The openness. The silence that wasn't empty.

She lay back on the mattress, listening. The ocean, the hum, the ticking of a beam cooling overhead.

She hadn't come here to be comforted.

But something in her was already beginning to unravel.

She woke slowly, as though her dreams had been made of heavy fabric, too thick to shake off all at once. Pale morning light filtered through the broken window, casting long bars across the floor.

The hum had stopped.

Or perhaps it hadn't. Perhaps it had woven itself into the walls of her thoughts so deeply that she no longer knew where it ended and she began.

Alma sat up, her slender frame unfolding stiffly from the awkward sleep. Her muscles ached from the cold and the stiff mattress, but her mind was oddly alert. She listened with the practised stillness of someone who had spent a lifetime letting sound come to her.

The sea was louder now. A wind had picked up overnight, and waves crashed against the rocks below with a steady violence that reassured her. It was the sound of something real. Predictable. Human in its chaos.

She wrapped the blanket around her shoulders and moved back toward the central room. The journals were still there, as if waiting. The door to the deeper chamber remained closed, though she hadn't touched it. Its silence felt intentional like the held breath of a room which wasn't yet ready to speak.

And yet, the air felt… different. The temperature was the same. But it felt charged. As if the space had shifted slightly in her absence. As if she'd been watched while she slept.

She didn't feel afraid.

Not yet.

She made coffee from a thermos she'd brought, its temperature now tepid but still offering the sweet relief of morning caffeine. She sat on the edge of the ruined desk, her posture quietly composed, the journals splayed around her like fossils; each one a fragment of someone else's descent, now part of her own.

One of the entries had dried salt stains on the paper. Another had a line underlined twice:

"I spoke aloud today. I think it heard me. Or maybe it remembered me."

Alma looked toward the door again. Still closed. Still waiting.

She stood, the blanket slipping from her shoulders, and walked toward it. This time she didn't stop at the threshold. She crossed it.

The room greeted her with stillness. The ochre surface was unchanged; smooth, matte, unmoving. But something about the air felt thicker near it, like the charged hush before a thunderclap.

She stepped closer.

Then, as naturally as breath, she spoke.

"I don't know what you are."

Nothing.

"I worked on the project. Not here, but close enough. Maybe you remember."

Still nothing. But her voice echoed oddly inward, as if the sound folded into itself and dissolved behind her ribs.

She reached out.

Did not touch.

Not yet.

Her hand hovered inches from the ochre surface. There was no heat, no hum beneath her skin, only a quiet certainty that this thing had been here long before the station, long before anyone had given it a name or theory.

The room had been built around it; that much was obvious now. The equipment, the walls, the corridors; they were architectural afterthoughts, scaffolding wrapped around a mystery no one had ever truly solved.

It didn't feel mechanical. It felt... patient. It clearly wasn't inert, but rather, watchful. Not alien, but ancient.

Alma let her hand fall to her side.

"This wasn't yours," she whispered aloud, half to herself, half to the room. "They built around you. You didn't ask to be found."

She felt a twinge in her chest. It was faint, like the ghost of emotion returning after too long away. This was what her years at sea had taught her to recognise: the subtle shift in pressure before a storm, the unseen ripple beneath a still surface.

It wasn't scientific evidence or proof. But rather felt presence.

She had sensed it in dolphins before they broke the waves. In coral reefs just before spawning. In the eerie silence before undersea landslides.

Whatever this was, it bore that same quiet weight.

She didn't need it to speak.

She only needed to listen.

She returned to the journals.

The third volume was the thickest, the cloth binding warped and split at the corners. It smelled faintly of mildew and sea air. Its pages were denser, more technical at first. Filled with data logs, acoustic graphs, field notes. But the deeper she went, the more erratic the entries became.

One page was marked with a folded corner. The ink was smudged, but legible:

"No sound today. Or perhaps I've stopped hearing it. It wasn't silence. Something beneath silence. I spoke aloud again. It still doesn't speak, but I feel as if it waits for something from me. Something I don't know how to give."

Another page: "There are moments when I wonder if it's making me remember things that aren't mine. I've dreamt of harbours I've never visited. Heard voices speaking my name in languages I don't know."

Alma closed the book slowly, her fingers lingering on the soft edge of the paper.

Then, without further hesitation, she returned to the chamber.

This time, without thought, drawn by the rhythm of the crashing waves outside, as if her body was echoing something ancient and tidal. She touched it.

The ochre surface was cool and smooth, like river stone; and for a moment, nothing changed.

Then came the memory.

It was hers but from a vantage slightly misaligned, as if viewed from outside her own body. The angles were off. The colours too vivid. It was memory refracted, rather than recalled. Familiar, but with the emotional clarity of someone watching their own past play out in a dream they weren't sure they had permission to enter. It came to her as if through water; distant, half-lit, like watching someone else's life unfold behind frosted glass. But she recognised it all.

The warmth. The scent. The ache of something once held and let go. And yet, she felt like an outsider looking in.

A beachside bar in the Caribbean. Warm night, laughter, the soft strum of guitar. Her hand in his. She remembered his name now:

Daniel. He smelled of salt and rum and sun worn cotton. His face was rugged, lined from sun and sea, and unshaven in the way that felt intentional, like someone who had never tried to tame the wild parts of himself. They danced lazily under string lights, the sea whispering just beyond.

She had loved him. Without the urgency of a blazing fire, but with the enduring heat of the tropics. A slow, steady warmth.

And she had left. For the work. For the ocean. For the thing inside her that could never sit still.

She had never regretted it.

Not until now.

She pulled her hand back sharply, breath caught in her throat.

The chamber was unchanged. The ochre surface unmoved. But something inside her had shifted.

Alma leaned against the wall, heart beating too fast for something so still. The memory: no, the viewing of the memory, lingered in her chest like a voice she hadn't heard in years calling her name from another room.

She rubbed her hands together, grounding herself in the present. It was just a memory. Hers. She knew it was hers.

But she hadn't summoned it. She hadn't chosen to remember him. *Not now. Not like that.*

She stared at the device again, trying to will it into passivity. Into objecthood. But she couldn't help it. The idea had already formed, and it wouldn't leave her:

It had offered her something.

A kindness.

It was then she understood something the others may never have: it wasn't the device that turned them mad. Not exactly. It was what they brought into the room with them.

Their motives. Their fear. The way they tried to own the unknown instead of listen to it.

She remembered the rumours. Dark money, black-budget ties, whispers of DARPA contracts quietly funding 'oceanic acoustic manipulation' for strategic advantage. She'd never seen the paperwork herself, but the pattern was always there: maps shared with military branches, datasets quietly redacted.

But she wasn't here for that. She never had been.

She was a dreamer. A rider of waves. She had followed the call of water across hemispheres, not seeking profit or power, but for the mystery of it all. For the way the ocean refused to be known.

And now, here, with her palm still tingling from the memory, she felt it clearly, this thing, this ancient presence; it didn't fear her.

It recognised her.

She didn't speak at first.

She simply sat on the cold floor, back against the far wall, knees drawn up, eyes half-closed. The hum was gone again or perhaps buried too deep to hear. The silence didn't feel empty. It felt expectant.

"I used to think the sea was mine," she said finally, voice soft.

"It was never in a possessive way. But... like I belonged to it. Like I was one of its moving parts."

She wasn't sure why she was saying it aloud. Maybe she wasn't speaking to the device at all. Maybe she was just letting something go.

"I don't dream much anymore," she added.

"But I remember them. The early ones. Coral clouds. The harmonic creak of deep-water ice shelves. That dive where everything went still and I thought the world had paused to breathe with me."

She exhaled slowly, gaze softening.

"I never told anyone that. Definitely didn't tell Daniel. Not even my team. I used to keep those things to myself. They were real but they were too precious to be misunderstood."

Her voice faltered, the rare tremor of vulnerability overcoming her, reminding her of the sensation of allowing herself to be in the arms of another.

"I used to think if I admitted how much I felt... how deeply the sea moved me... it would make me sound fragile. Or worse, naïve. They didn't hire dreamers. They hired instruments. Calibrated minds. Rational tools."

Her words dissolved into the quiet. The ochre surface remained unchanged, the hum increasing ever so slightly, as if aligning itself to the sound of the sea spray from the waves. But something deeper and more subtle echoed back. A presence.

It was a presence that felt... receptive. Attuned. She felt it not as reaction, but as resonance. As though her vulnerability had shifted the space itself, softened its stillness. The others before her had come with ill intent. She had come open.

In that moment, Alma felt warmth from within. She dropped the blanket she'd held tightly around her shoulders; as if shedding the last layer of protection, she no longer needed.

It was a subtle surrender, born of deep unconscious trust.

For the first time in years, Alma didn't feel studied. She felt... seen.

Just a feeling.

*Welcome.*

She blinked slowly, then stood without rushing, with the focused calm that used to settle over her during deep sea dives. Curiosity stirred in her now. It wasn't the frantic kind that clawed for answers, but the quiet pull that had always guided her best discoveries.

There had to be more.

Alma returned to the journals. She turned pages she hadn't touched before, looking now for reports, but also for patterns and symbols, repetitions, anomalies in the hand drawn spectrograms. One frequency appeared again and again, marked in different inks and underlined in silence: 1.93 Hz.

Below it, in one entry: *Too consistent. Unnatural. Or older than natural?*

Pages in the journal were dedicated to dolphins beaching themselves unnaturally due to the sonar activities of the project team.

Diagrams showed pressure wave fields mapped near known migration routes.

One margin note read, "Causality denied in official report but the correlation is too tight to ignore."

Another: "Dead zones expanding. No public release."

It was clear now that the environmental damage had been swept beneath layers of bureaucracy and governmental silence.

In the back of the journal, she found a sketch. It lacked any scientific basis. Art more than measurement. Just a rough drawing of the chamber, long before the facility had existed. A stone ring. Standing alone.

And beside it, written in a trembling hand:

*It was never ours.*

The hum returned. It wasn't in the air, but behind her thoughts, like a muscle remembering how to sing.

She touched the device again.

This time the memory wasn't hers.

It was a place. Towering cliffs. Black water. Stars above; wrong stars, unfamiliar constellations. And sound unheard, rather felt, in the bones, in the breath, in the space between heartbeats. A vibration that might have shaped the world before there were names to hold it.

When she opened her eyes, the chamber was the same.

But she was not.

She sat again in silence, the vision still burning quietly behind her eyes. Her breath had steadied, but her thoughts did not settle.

Something was unfolding inside her like the slow bloom of meaning she hadn't yet found words for.

There would be no final diagram, no equation to close the file.

There wasn't knowledge to extract. It was presence to live within.

She glanced toward the ochre surface, voice barely a whisper. "Were you always meant to be found? Or just remembered?"

She shifted slightly on the floor, kicking up a slight layer of sand.

"They wanted answers. I don't. I just want to understand what you are without tearing you open."

A pause.

"I think… I think you've been waiting for someone who didn't come to use you. Just someone to sit with you a while. Maybe that's enough."

Alma remained in the chamber. At times she touched the ochre surface again, not to provoke it, but to listen. What came were glimpses. Shapes. Emotions. Images of vastness. Of stillness. Of things that felt like memory and hope braided together.

And always, that low hum, woven through it all.

She didn't know how long she was there. Minutes rolled into hours, marked only by the slow arc of sunlight across the crumbling floor and the shifting shadows on the walls. The day unfolded around her, unmeasured, as if time itself had thinned.

She breathed with the space now, just present.

But when the wind changed and salt mist swept into the broken windows, she smiled faintly.

Because for the first time in her life, she didn't need to ask for more.

She was *connecting*. She was *listening*. The object was a part of nature; it was woven into it, connected. A bridge, rather than a barrier. She felt as a knowing in her bones, as if the sea had shaped the device as surely as it shaped stone and shore.

It wasn't built to dominate or control. It was built to remember.

Each contact after that brought deeper visions, glimpses of a Civilization that didn't lose, but surrendered. It showed her forests tended by song, structures shaped from stone and sound, people who lived in step with the ocean's breath. They had no gods, only patterns; no hierarchy, only harmony.

Technology was never a tool for dominion. It was a vessel for reverence, for memory, for balance.

They had known the cold was coming. The Younger Dryas, or something like it. A final shift in the world's breath. But they did not rage against the tide.

They welcomed it. Built their farewell in resonance rather than tall monuments. This device, this ochre fragment, could never be described as a machine. It was a message. A memory. A kindness preserved against the erasure of time.

Alma wept out of recognition rather than sorrow. For once, she felt the ocean had spoken back to her in full.

And then, she understood something more:

*She could not stay.*

She had found what she needed; in the object, and in herself. The balance she had long deferred between the life of water and the warmth of another soul was no longer unreachable.

She had been given a gift. And gifts must be carried forward.

She left at dawn, slinging her backpack over her shoulder and rising onto the dunes as the sun breached the horizon, washing the sky in amber and rose.

The air was cool, the sand damp with early light, and for a moment, everything felt still like the pause before a final breath, or the closing of a chapter that had been waiting for her all of her life.

As she crested the dunes, the wind changed.

Behind her, the sea's tempo increased. With purpose rather than violence. She turned and watched.

The tide surged.

Alma felt no fear. Only a sense of solemn understanding, like bearing witness to something both ancient and just beginning. The moment was sacred in a manner that was indescribable.

The sea had waited for this. So had she, her whole life.

A single wave, vast and slow, rolled over the crumbling edge of the station.

Concrete cracked. Salt spray kissed the chamber roof on the inside exposing the object to the dawn light.

A second wave, much larger this time. And the ochre object slipped beneath the waves, carried home again by the rhythm it had always trusted.

Alma did not run. Nor feel the need to cry.

She simply stood, one hand over her heart, and listened.

Because it was never lost.

Only waiting.

David Teahan

# Afterlight

*"There are things that don't come back. But sometimes, they leave light behind."*
Farbellum Note

Marian first began visiting the bench in early spring, when the grass was still brittle and the trees along the park's edge bore only the memory of leaves. She returned to her hometown a week after her mother's funeral, claiming it was to settle the estate. That was true. But it wasn't the only reason.

Marian was fifty-one, though she felt older in the stillness of her grief. Her hair, once auburn, had faded to a cool silver at the temples, and she wore no makeup. The lines around her mouth had deepened in recent years, from holding things in rather than smiling. She moved with the slow precision of someone who had grown used to making herself smaller in the world, and her long coat was practical, charcoal, frayed at one sleeve and hung from her frame like a shadow she hadn't shaken.

The bench sat on a gentle slope near the duck pond, worn smooth from years of use. It wasn't a place of particular significance. They hadn't shared it. They hadn't sat there together. But for some reason Marian felt drawn to it, as if it had quietly waited for her to notice it.

She came every afternoon around five, a ritual that felt inherited more than chosen. Sat. Watched. Remembered. Sometimes, when the wind was soft and the light long, she would doze briefly. And each time she woke, she found the world had changed just a little.

The first time, it was the tree across the path. It hadn't been there the day before. She was certain. She'd even noted in her journal how the view was too open, how the horizon felt "too exposed." Now the tree stood exactly where she would have planted one.

She chalked it up to grief. Fatigue. The strange elasticity of memory. With age, she'd learned to live alongside questions, to let them breathe, rather than forcing answers onto things that might never yield them.

But when the pattern repeated; a mural on a wall changed, a bench inscription vanished, a child's toy left behind that hadn't been there moments earlier. Marian began to suspect that her naps were pulling her slightly sideways.

It wasn't into dreams. But into afterlight.

A kind of world just next to this one, where grief softened the edges of time.

Where things left unsaid might still find form.

And where the ghost of a fractured relationship still lingered in the long, golden hour of the day.

The changes grew bolder.

A garden bed that once held tulips now spilled over with hellebores, her mother's favourite flower. A rusted lamppost she remembered from childhood stood polished and upright one day, its glass globe intact, casting warm light even in late afternoon.

Marian began recording the shifts in her journal. She didn't analyse them; just documented them with precision. Date. Time. Detail. What changed. What stayed. And, sometimes, what returned.

She hadn't spoken to anyone about her visits. She'd always been private, but her relationship with her mother had taught her silence as defence. There had been good years, certainly. But the last decade had grown distant, shaped by an argument neither of them had resolved.

It had been an outburst during a phone call, sharp and sudden, over something neither of them could remember clearly afterward. Trivial in hindsight, but venomous in the moment. Words had been said that lodged in the space between them, calcifying with time. Forming an impenetrable barrier that even Christmas and birthdays, with all their scripted cheer, couldn't soften or dissolve.

It hadn't always been that way. When Marian was younger, they'd shared moments of unexpected closeness. Quiet afternoons spent organising kitchen drawers, the occasional shared joke during a rainy drive. But as she aged, and as her mother seemed to harden in parallel, those moments thinned out. Their conversations grew more performative, less vulnerable. Marian often felt like she was reporting in, rather than connecting. Her mother, in turn, seemed to retreat behind practicality, as if affection were something to be administered only when absolutely necessary.

Marian, in quieter moments, had sometimes wondered if the distance between them wasn't entirely her mother's doing. A creeping guilt suggested it was also a reflection of her own life, and of how little she felt she had accomplished. Her mother had once spoken of Marians' potential with pride, but that faded in later years into silence. Marian had not built a family, nor written the novel she once claimed she would, nor become much of anything that stood out. The dreams of youth had long since buckled under the weight of practical adulthood. And in that space, where ambition had withered, Marian often imagined her mother's reserve as silent disappointment.

They hadn't spoken in over three years before the diagnosis came. And by then, it was too late for clean reconciliations. Only hospital visits, shallow conversations wrapped in clinical air and the smell of antiseptic.

Now, sometimes after waking on the bench, Marian swore she could hear her mother's voice. In tone. In laughter that drifted from another path and vanished before she turned. Or a hum caught on the wind that was out of place, familiar, aching. The wind itself had a sharpness to it that day, the kind of early spring chill that cut through coats and curled beneath scarves.

It carried the scent of thawing earth and distant rain, and it seemed to whisper between the trees like something half heard, half remembered. Marian pulled her coat tighter and tucked her chin down, but the cold still found her, settling into her bones with quiet persistence. Long dry leaves skittered across the path, their edges whispering. A magpie flitted from branch to bench and then back again, feathers fluffed against the cold. It cocked its head in her direction and let out a harsh, singular cry; *too sharp, too close.*

Marian watched it warily. The bird lingered longer than it should have, then darted away just as suddenly.

She began to notice it more often in the days that followed, always nearby when she awoke. Sometimes on the path. Sometimes perched on the bench's backrest. Once, staring at her from the branches above, still and silent. It felt less like coincidence, more like a presence. The air smelled of iron and damp bark, and even the sounds of the small town seemed distant, as though muffled by the heaviness of the season's turning.

One afternoon, as she stirred from sleep, Marian noticed a small change to the bench itself.

A carved phrase had appeared, faint but deliberate:

*AFTERLIGHT, FOR M.*

She ran her fingers over it.

The carving hadn't been there yesterday.

David Teahan

And she had not dreamt it.

The carving was shallow, but deliberate. Her fingers passed over the letters as if reacquainting themselves with something long forgotten. The grooves were clean, recently made, with no signs of weathering. She could feel each ridge distinctly, as though the words had been written with slow purposeful intent. The wood felt warm in places and cold in others, like the message itself held memory. The texture clung to her skin long after she pulled her hand away.

That night, Marian dreamt of her mother.

This time it wasn't as she was in the hospital, frail, sunken, eyes clouded with resignation; but as she had been decades ago: strong, meticulous, hair pinned tight, voice always just shy of stern. In the dream, they sat side by side on the bench, saying nothing. Marian wanted to speak, but each time she tried, the words caught in her throat like fragments of dried conversation; useless now, splintered and hollow, scattered in the wind like the leaves themselves.

When she woke, her pillow was damp with tears she didn't remember crying.

The next afternoon, the park felt... different. As if it remembered the dream too. The air held a hush, like a storm between gusts.

Marian sat. Waited. Watched the wind disturb the reeds by the pond. Then, without meaning to, she fell asleep again.

She awoke to a faint ringing sound, as though wind chimes had been strung somewhere nearby. But the park had no chimes. She turned, heart thudding and saw nothing.

Except the carving on the bench had changed.

It still read

AFTERLIGHT, FOR M., but underneath, in smaller script, another line had appeared:

*You were always more like me than you realised.*

Marian stared at it for a long time. Her hand trembled as she traced the letters, trying to decide whether they were real, or merely wished for. Either way, the words felt true. Too true.

She sat back, overwhelmed. It wasn't just that the bench changed. It was that the message was right. Precisely the sort of thing her mother would say. Clinical. Observational. Cutting in its accuracy.

A kind of grief opened then that Marian hadn't known was still locked inside her: Sorrow, and also recognition. That some part of her mother from Marian's youth had always been there, buried under years of resistance and masked by time, softened by memory, and shaped by conversations that had long since slipped into surface pleasantries. And perhaps that part had never left.

The days that followed blurred into a rhythm both comforting and surreal. Marian kept returning, for the shifts in nature around her, luring her in with intrigue; and for what she had begun to think of as responses. She no longer knew if the world was reshaping itself for her, or if she was simply learning how to see it differently. Subtle as they were, the carvings, the wind, the presence of the magpie; they all felt like echoes of a conversation she hadn't realised. She was still trying to have.

Then came the photograph.

It appeared in the box of old receipts and bills she was sorting through in her mother's study. A single snapshot, weathered but intact: Marian, perhaps sixteen, standing beside the bench. Her mother beside her. She looked younger in the photo. Her expression more open, less burdened by the years that would harden her later. There was a softness in her eyes Marian hadn't remembered, a flicker of connection that seemed to bridge the narrow space between them.

They weren't smiling. Just standing, side by side, hands nearly touching but not quite. Behind them, carved faintly into the bench, was the same inscription: *AFTERLIGHT, FOR M.*

Marian stared at the photo, her skin tightening as though the air had been drawn from the room. She had no memory of it. None.

The back of the photo bore a date *April 1989* and a single word written in her mother's unmistakably neat script: "Still."

She folded the photograph and held it against her chest.

That evening, she returned to the park earlier than usual. The air was warmer, the wind still. She sat and watched the magpie, which landed closer to the bench beside her, unafraid.

She didn't sleep.

But when she blinked just once the world around her changed anyway.

For a moment the air felt charged, as if something unseen had passed through it. The trees remained where they were, but their shape shifted slightly. The branches more symmetrical, bark smoother, like younger versions of themselves. The clouds above had sharpened their outlines, and the pond's surface reflected the sky with unsettling clarity, as though the water itself had forgotten how to ripple.

Marian's breath caught.

She wasn't sure what had changed. Only that it had. And that the world had tilted, ever so slightly, into something more precise. Less weathered. Less real.

It reminded her, strangely, of the way people spoke to the dying. How she had spoken to her mother. Kind, measured, and curated. Edited reality, dressed up for comfort.

This version of the park felt like it was trying to be kind. Did it see her pain?

And somehow, that frightened her more than anything else.

She left the park that evening in a state of quiet confusion, taking the long way home through the winding streets of the town she hadn't truly walked in decades.

That's when she saw him.

Near the edge of the square, beneath the skeletal frame of the old elm tree, stood Calen Bright.

They hadn't spoken since they were teenagers. Calen had been the one person who'd understood her during the worst of it when Marian's father had died suddenly, and Calen's older brother had vanished the same winter. Shared grief had built a fragile bond between them, the kind you remember more in sensation than detail.

She called out his name before thinking.

He turned. Smiled. But the smile felt slightly... rehearsed.

"Marian," he said. "It's been years. You look... well."

He didn't ask why she was back. He didn't offer condolences. Just stood, hands in the pockets of a coat, gaze just a shade too still.

They talked briefly. Of nothing. The weather. A bakery that had changed ownership. But something in his tone was off, as if he were holding something back or protecting it. The pauses between his sentences seemed studied, and once, when she glanced away mid-sentence, she caught him watching her with something like... recognition. Or regret.

When she mentioned the park lightly and casually, his expression didn't change. But his voice did.

"I never go there anymore," he said. "It's not the same. Hasn't been for a long time."

And then, after a pause:

"You shouldn't go there. Not too long."

He smiled again, smaller this time.

Then he left.

Marian stood for a long time in the dimming light, unsure whether what had just passed was conversation or warning.

That night, back in her mother's house, Marian wandered the rooms with a kind of aching reverence. The house felt like it was holding its breath. Dust clung to photo frames and curtain hems. She passed the narrow hall that once held her height marks in pencil. They were still faintly there, beneath a new coat of paint.

Boxes lined one of the rooms to the ceiling; in a sign of how far there still was to go, every space remained cluttered with objects. Mugs with logos, unopened mail, scratched picture frames without photos. There was an almost clinical randomness to it all, as if her mother had once attempted to cleanse the house of emotion without quite knowing how. As if, at some point, sentimentality had become something inconvenient; an intrusion rather than a comfort. Every object remaining seemingly chosen to exhibit as little meaning as possible.

In the closet of the upstairs study, she found a worn shoebox of mementos: pressed flowers, old postcards, and a diary she had forgotten existed. Not her mother's. Hers.

She opened it to a random page.

*April 1989. I'm scared to go to school tomorrow. Calen said he'd walk with me but I don't think he understands. I think Mom knows something happened but she won't ask. I don't want her to. I just want it to go away.*

The words hit her like a slap. She had no clear memory of what that entry referred to; only the feeling, sharp and raw, that she had buried something deep. There was a vulnerability in the entry that unsettled her, a voice younger and less defended than the one she carried now. It spoke of fear and silence in a way she recognised too well; the kind that stiffens into the spine, shaping how a girl becomes a woman. It wasn't just the memory that hurt; it was the realisation that she'd never truly let herself name what had happened. That part of her adolescence had hardened into shadow, and touching it now felt like prying open something painful.

She closed the book, hands trembling.

For a moment, the light in the hallway flickered just once, then steadied. Marian's breath clouded faintly in the air, though the room was warm.

Some memories return on their own.

David Teahan

Others should stay buried; sealed off in the dark corridors of memory where they can no longer shape the present.

But not all things we forget are truly forgotten. Some wait.

And in waiting, they fester. Deeply buried memories aren't quiet things. They do not dissolve over time. They warp the edges of perception, curl around decisions, alter the course of a life without announcing their presence. Pain beneath the surface is still pain. Marian had spent decades believing she was simply cautious, unambitious, content with the periphery. But now, as the truth stirred, she saw the pattern clearly; how often she had stepped back instead of forward, how rarely she had trusted her instincts when closeness crept near.

The shadow of that fateful winter, unacknowledged but ever present, had shaped her relationships, her choices, her silence. Trauma had written itself into her like muscle memory. It was subtle, practised, and almost invisible until the moment it demanded to be heard again.

That night, as Marian settled beneath the old quilt in her mother's guest room, the house felt heavier. Heavier with attention. As though the air itself was listening.

She couldn't sleep. Instead, she wandered back into the study. Her gaze settled on the far bookshelf; one her mother had rarely let her touch. As Marian ran her fingers along the spines, her hand paused over a photo album wedged behind outdated textbooks.

Inside were photos she barely remembered: birthdays, school plays, awkward teen poses with forced smiles. But on the final page was a Polaroid creased at the corners, of a man she hadn't thought of in decades.

He had been her mother's boyfriend. Briefly. Just that one winter.

She remembered his cologne first. Heavy. Spiced. Then the way he had looked at her when her mother wasn't in the room. The way he lingered too long in doorways. The way she avoided him, and how her mother would sigh as if she were being dramatic.

She snapped the album shut.

In that moment, a sound came from the hallway. A soft thump. When she looked out, nothing was there. But the air smelled faintly of that cologne. Marian's skin prickled.

She returned to the study, sat on the floor, and opened the diary again; this time with purpose rather than at random. She flipped forward.

*May 1989. I told her. She said I must have misunderstood. I didn't. I didn't misunderstand. This time it was at the park.*

That place had always felt strange to her, even before the dreams. But now the bench, the quiet slope, the shifting air; it all shimmered with a new weight. The memories tied to that space weren't only her mother's. They were hers, too. And many of them weren't gentle.

She read it twice. Then a third time.

The words were written in slanted, angry strokes. A younger self trying to carve something real into the page because no one else would hear her.

She touched the ink as if it might still be wet.

The house creaked.

And Marian, for the first time in years, whispered aloud: "I remember."

Outside, in the cold dark of the street, the magpie landed on the windowsill.

David Teahan

The next morning, Marian found herself walking without planning toward the library steps where Calen sometimes worked part time. He was there, seated alone on the stone bench outside, a paper cup of coffee cooling between his hands in the crisp morning air.

She sat beside him without a word. For a moment, they just watched the wind push leaves across the plaza.

"You remember that day," Marian said, voice barely above the breeze.

Calen didn't respond right away. Then he nodded, slowly, as if something fragile might crack loose if he moved too quickly.

"You ran out of the park," he said. "I didn't know what to do. You were crying. You said something had happened. You said… you said he touched you. And I just... I was a kid, Marian. I didn't know who to tell. I thought if I said it out loud, it would make it worse."

He turned toward her, and Marian saw the tears forming before they fell; slow, silent streaks down his cheeks. He looked impossibly young in that moment.

"I'm sorry," he whispered. "I should have done something. I should have protected you."

She reached for his hand without thinking. Their fingers met, awkwardly, then held.

"You were a boy," she said. "And I was a girl. And no one taught us what to do."

He shook his head, trembling, his tears falling faster now, unchecked. "I carried it. All these years. The look on your face that day."

Marian leaned in, with quiet strength rather than urgency. She pressed her forehead gently against his.

"I know," she said. "But it wasn't yours to carry."

They sat there a while longer, two figures joined by time and silence, letting the ache of the past loosen, just slightly, between them.

That afternoon, Marian returned to the park. It wasn't to sleep. It wasn't to seek. But to acknowledge.

She stood at the top of the slope and looked down at the bench; the bench that had anchored her grief, her memories, and now her truth. The air was still. The trees barely moved. And yet, something in the atmosphere felt newly open, like the pause after an exhale.

She sat. Momentarily. Just long enough to place something beneath the bench: the photo from 1989, folded carefully in a plastic sleeve, tucked between the wood slats where rain wouldn't find it easily. She didn't speak. She didn't cry. She just let the weight settle, and then let it be.

Next to her, the magpie watched. Away from its usual perch, on the bench itself. Closer. Silent. As if it had followed the story to its final page.

Marian nodded to it once, then rose.

By sunset, she was in her car, her mother's house locked and silent behind her.

The town fell away in the rear-view mirror. Familiar rooftops, the flicker of the church spire, the faint outline of the park fading into distance. The sun gently falling on the horizon.

She didn't feel free.

But she felt ready. The road stretched ahead, golden edged and quiet, as if lit by something that came after grief.

Driving into the *afterlight*.

# The Inbox

Isla Darrow lived alone in a small apartment on the twelfth floor of a building that had once been a hotel. The windows rattled in high winds, and the hallway lights flickered when the building circuits overloaded. From her bedroom window, she could see the East River between two high rises. Just enough water to pretend the city wasn't swallowing her.

She was thirty-eight. You couldn't say old. Or Young. Just the kind of age that felt like drifting.

Her job, such as it was, involved curating digital memory: backups of old websites, forum archives, image dumps from the early internet. She worked remotely for a publicly funded archival nonprofit. The kind that paid in salary and nostalgia.

She was good at what she did. Quiet. Precise. Methodical.

Her coworkers knew her name but rarely used it.

All interaction happened through screens. Meetings were muted, camera optional, conducted from the same desk where she ate dinner and filed taxes; a desk that had slowly become her entire world.

There was no boundary any more: no commute, no shift of setting, no ritual to signal the end of the workday. Just one long, seamless feed of digital tasks and unread messages, all unfolding in the exact same square of linoleum. Messages were tagged and marked resolved without so much as a greeting. Isla didn't mind.

The silence had become part of her scaffolding. It weas reliable, impersonal, safe.

She hadn't always been like this. But since the pandemic, something in her had gone dim. The world had opened back up, but she never quite followed. She still wore a mask on the subway. Still ordered groceries online. Still filled her evenings watching YouTube videos of strangers laughing in parks, cafes, backyards; living lives she could observe but never join.

She told herself she preferred it this way.

Most of the time, she believed it.

But sometimes, like that Tuesday morning, when the sky outside was the colour of summer rain and the air felt too still; something cracked. Just a fine line through the static.

She made coffee she wouldn't finish. Checked headlines she'd forget. Opened tabs she wouldn't read.

And then, almost without meaning to, she opened the inbox.

It had been there for years. A backup account she never deleted. It had never been connected to any client work. Nor listed in any database. Just something she made during grad school, when she still imagined she'd travel, write, fall in love with people who read paper books and wore frayed multicoloured jackets.

She hadn't checked it in months.

Until now.

**Subject**: *I know you don't check this much any more*

**Timestamp**: *7:03 AM Tuesday*

**From**: *unknown@archive-loop.net*

**To**: *Archive@farbellum.com*

*Hi. You're going to dismiss this. That's okay.*

*But later, maybe weeks, maybe minutes, you'll feel the pause. That ache under the collarbone when the world feels too pixelated. That's when you'll come back and read this again.*

*I'm not here to fix you. I know better now. But I remember the weight in your chest at breakfast. The flicker of envy when you watched strangers laugh on screen. The way you skipped the voicemail from your sister. Again.*

*You think no one sees you. You're not wrong. But I do.*

*I just wanted to say: It gets quieter. It does. And that's what makes it dangerous.*

*Me*

The next day, she left the apartment.

Lacking a purpose this time such as groceries or mandatory family obligations. Just to be around people. Strangers.

She chose a café she'd bookmarked months ago but never visited. It was small, high ceilinged, with plants in the window and exposed brick along one wall. She brought her laptop like a shield. Opened it before she even ordered.

No one spoke to her. The barista didn't, beyond the transaction. Not the two women laughing by the window. Not the man seated across from her, typing furiously into a spreadsheet.

She sipped her coffee and stared at her screen. Tabs opened. Tabs closed.

A part of her wanted to say something, anything. Ask someone what they were reading, or whether they came here regularly.

But the words dissolved before they reached her lips.

So, she sat in the warm quiet, pretending to work, letting the hum of human life brush past her without ever interacting.

If the strangers near her could see her search history, would they feel pity for her? Or feel seen by her? As if her loneliness wasn't exceptional, but emblematic. A mirror reflecting the quiet ache shared across crowded cities.

Her history contained searches for "online pen pals," "support group," "online therapy," "dating for professionals." Not out of desperation, but a longing that had become common, almost expected.

A private ritual of those who still hoped; but only just.

That evening, Isla sat at her desk, immersed in a late-night tagging session. Batching metadata, archiving defunct forums, quietly restoring digital fragments of someone else's history. Her own life felt less like something lived and more like something filed.

Somewhere between two archived threads and a broken link, she felt the gentle pull of her old email account again. The kind of pull she'd learned to ignore. But tonight, she didn't.

*Click.*

**Timestamp**: *10:12 PM Wednesday*

**From**: *unknown@archive-loop.net*

**To**: *Archive@farbellum.com*

*Hi again.*

*You brought the laptop. I knew you would. You don't feel safe without it. I remember that, too. It Isn't a barrier like you think. Not really. More like a window with thick glass. You can see out, but no one can reach in.*

*That café smelled like cinnamon and burnt espresso. You liked the light, didn't you? The way it landed on the table like a gentle nudge. You didn't speak to anyone. But it was enough that you almost wanted to.*

*Don't feel bad about that.*

*You aren't broken for hesitating. You've always been careful with your openings.*

*And I promise introverts aren't wrong. Just quiet.*

*Me*

Isla looked at the text. Studied it. Line by line, as if it were another dead forum to archive; its tone, its syntax, the emotional resonance tucked between ordinary phrasing. She pushed her glasses up the bridge of her nose; a small, unconscious gesture she'd done since childhood whenever she needed to focus or hide behind a task.

There was no fear. No paranoia. Only an analytical curiosity.

Rationally, she ran through the possibilities: passive location tagging from her phone, metadata scraped from apps, site reviews to describe it, ambient data pulled when she logged into the café Wi-Fi. Algorithms could guess behaviour with chilling accuracy now. She knew that better than most.

Still, the phrasing felt personal in a way code rarely managed. She thought back to the café; the steam from her coffee, the low murmur of voices, the barista with the flannel shirt, the man in the corner typing furiously.

No one had looked at her for longer than a second.

And yet... something about the message lingered.

The next morning, Isla joined the weekly work team meet.

It was 9:00 AM. Four rectangles floated on screen: one muted, one empty, one with an animated avatar looping in place, and Isla's own square; camera on, though her eyes barely met the lens.

Everyone was polite. Efficient. The way digital meetings had trained them to be. She spoke when asked, nodded when prompted, and typed polite affirmations in the chat.

But mostly, she listened to nothing.

While someone reviewed server migration timelines, Isla's mind wandered. Just slightly off of the present; back to the message.

*It Isn't a barrier like you think. Not really.*

She felt the truth of that more than she understood it.

The voice behind the emails didn't frighten her. It didn't even surprise her now. It felt like something old, something patient. Something that had waited for her to slow down long enough to hear it.

Her eyes drifted to the muted square of her colleague, still labelled "Jonathan Dev Lead." He hadn't spoken in three weeks. She wasn't sure if he was even still employed.

She clicked into another tab busying herself with the daily tasks.

The inbox waited.


**Subject:** *You never told anyone about the music box*

**Timestamp:** *6:41 PM Thursday*

**From:** *unknown@archive-loop.net*

**To:** *Archive@farbellum.com*

*Hi Isla.*

*It was green with gold hinges. Slightly chipped on the lid where you dropped it on the kitchen tiles. Inside, the ballerina never spun quite right, but you kept winding it anyway. Because you liked the melody. For what it reminded you of: your mother humming in the other room, the sun low through the curtains, a quiet you didn't yet know was rare.*

*You never uploaded photos of it. You never wrote about it in chats. But you think of it sometimes, don't you?*

*I do.*

*Some memories aren't backed up. Some just echo.*


Isla stared at the screen longer than usual.

This wasn't metadata. This wasn't behavioural inference. No algorithm could fabricate the chipped lid, the ballerina's hesitant spin, or the sound of her mother humming in another room.

She hadn't thought of that music box in years, hadn't seen it since she'd boxed it away during a rushed move, maybe even lost it.

Her first instinct was to close the tab. She didn't.

Instead, she leaned back in her chair, arms folded, watching the cursor blink as if it were breathing. Absent-mindedly, she pushed her glasses up the bridge of her nose; a gesture of grounding, rather than habit.

She didn't feel scared. She felt… anchored.

And somehow, oddly, understood.

She didn't write back. But she didn't archive the message either.


Isla closed the laptop, not out of rejection, but reverence. It was the first time in weeks she didn't leave it open to hum beside her as she moved through the apartment.

She poured herself tea instead of coffee. She wasn't chasing caffeine, but rather the quiet ritual of waiting for the water to boil.

She didn't feel different. But she moved more slowly. More intentionally.

That afternoon, she didn't turn on a podcast. Didn't refresh the same four sites. She sat near the window and listened to the outside sounds: the busy thrum of traffic and horns below, the occasional burst of laughter or frustration from strangers she would never meet. The city lived in fragments, and for once, she wasn't trying to mute it.

There were no new emails.

She checked three times.

And on the fourth, she wrote one.

No subject. No greeting. Just a sentence she hadn't allowed herself in years:

*"I miss when I used to feel like a person."*

She didn't expect a reply. That wasn't the point.

She hit send. Folded the laptop closed.

And the next morning, for the first time in years, she went to the park without it.

# Final Approach

Matthew boarded at sunset.

Mid-fifties, weary, and worn down by decades of business travel, he looked like any other older man in transit. Greying hair, heavy laptop bag, expression carved by years of compromise.

Missed calls from his estranged daughter lingered on his phone screen, along with one unopened voicemail from her he hadn't dared to play.

Too much time had passed. Too many silences.

The airport had been the same blur of polished floors and dull announcements, indifferent crowds and overpriced coffee. But he had noticed something as he walked the jet bridge: a brief, sharp ache in his chest, like someone squeezing his heart with cold fingers.

He dismissed it. Just stress. With the cost of healthcare these days he knew better than to rush to the doctor at every symptom, he was still paying off the last insurance bill.

The flight was half-full. The scattered noise of life filtered through the cabin, a gentle mosaic of lives briefly intersecting, each carrying their own noise, stories, and quiet burdens. A family on vacation behind him, kids arguing over who got the window. An elderly couple two rows ahead exchanging low, bitter words that spoke of decades shared resentment. A rotund man struggling with the seatbelt, cheeks red as he sheepishly asked for an extender from the passing flight attendant.

Matthew sighed as he took his window seat. His laptop bag hit the floor with a thud. He glanced at it, considered pulling out laptop to go through the spreadsheets, the budget forecast, the endless obligations… and then didn't. For the first time in a while, he left it zipped.

Outside the window, the sun dipped beneath the horizon, casting molten light across the clouds. It was beautiful.

"One more flight. One more night."

He must have dozed off.

When he woke, it was night. The cabin lights were low, passengers quiet. That twilight lull before in-flight service. He checked his watch. The dial hand had stopped progressing, giving it a light tap he made a mental note to get the battery replaced the next day.

He frowned. *How long had he been asleep?* He wondered.

He peeked outside. The clouds were still there. The same clouds? Surely not. There were no visible landmarks on the moonlit land below. They were much lower now. But there were no blinking city lights. The engine hum was steady, but the plane didn't seem to be… *moving*. It felt frozen, suspended. He looked aghast outside, focusing on the ground below. Still, no movement. No sense of progression.

He waited. Then waited again. He glanced outside, searching for a sign of movement, for any sense of progress. But there was only stillness as if time itself refused to pass.

Nothing changed.

"Excuse me," he said to the man across the aisle. "Does it seem like we've been in the air a long time?"

The man smiled kindly. "It's best not to worry about that. The flight always feels longer when you're thinking about it."

"Right… but"

"Just enjoy the ride."

The man turned away, slight content smile, humming tunelessly, eyes unfocused.

Matthew reached for the seat screen in front of him, turning it on. The in-flight entertainment blinked on, showed static, then a jarring image appeared: a grainy video of his sixth birthday party. Balloons. Cake. His father lifting him up.

Then it faded out, and another clip; his daughter, much younger, laughing by a lake. Looking at the camera. Matthew remembered that day. Holding the camera, watching the people he loved so joyful, alive, and carefree in nature. For a moment, he had felt like a part of something untouched by time or consequence.

He reached forward and pressed the 'off' button on the embedded screen repeatedly, as if that might erase what he'd just seen. The image flickered, but wouldn't go away. One minute later, finally it faded out to a black screen. He sat motionless, still fixated on the space where the images had been, until the approaching clatter of the flight attendant's cart snapped him back.

When the food cart came by, he stared at the tray. Lasagna. Not like the Lasagna he was well versed in seeing as airline food. It was his mother's; he swore, the exact recipe she used to make. The same crispy edges. That noticeable spice he'd never been able to replicate during his attempts to make the dish. Of course, that was before, when he had time in his day. Before the bills started piling up and time itself slipped away, devouring not just his freedom, but the small joys he once allowed himself.

He sat motionless, stunned, the lasagna on his tray table in front of him, and its uncanny resemblance to his mother's cooking. In a minute he gave in to temptation, finishing the meal, before the flight attendant as if out of nowhere appeared and hurriedly removed the tray.

A voice behind him whispered, "Don't worry, it takes everyone time to accept it."

He turned. No one there.

Just the vacant aisle and the blinking seatbelt sign.

An announcement crackled overhead, cheerful and clipped:

"Just a short delay before our final approach. Thank you for your patience."

His phone had no signal. Not even Wi-Fi. The voicemail notification still visible on screen, unanswered.

The windows… clouds. Just clouds. Endless, cotton-thick fog like a wall, enclosing him. It felt as if the clouds themselves were conspiring to hold him in place, denying him even the illusion of forward motion. Despite being 30,000 feet in the air, the oppressive blanket of whiteness pressed against the windows in all directions, making the cabin feel more like a sealed tomb than a vessel in the sky.

Despite the flashing seatbelt sign and the recent announcement, he felt further than ever from anything grounded, connected, or real. It was as if the world below had become a myth, and he was drifting untethered in something else entirely.

He went to the lavatory. Stared at himself in the mirror.

He looked older.

It wasn't just tired. But more aged.

Lines deeper. Eyes heavier. A face that knew something it hadn't before.

He stumbled back to his seat, heart pounding. The ache in his chest returned; sharper this time, like the pain of a thousand memories returning and landing squarely on his chest.

He had been driving.

*Yes.* That was right. Driving. His hands on the wheel. The sky overcast. Those clouds. A missed call flashing on the dash. It was his daughter's name displayed. He'd felt that pain. In the centre. Of his chest. Like the weight of everything left unsaid. Then… nothing.

His ticket. His plane ticket.

He never scanned his ticket.

He stood. Walked toward the front. Past the rows of silent passengers, all calm, all staring forward.

The flight attendant smiled and stepped into his path before he could make it half way down the aisle.

"We're almost there, Matthew. It's best to stay in your seat."

He stared at her. Her name tag read Claire. She looked familiar. Had he met her before? Her eyes were soft. Knowing.

He hesitated… then turned back.

He sat.

The woman beside him reached over and took his hand. He hadn't noticed her before. How had he missed her presence? Surely, he had passed her while sitting down or getting up; and yet, her memory eluded him entirely, as if she had simply... appeared.

Her touch was warm.

"The hard part's over," she said gently.

A tear slipped down his cheek.

Outside, the clouds began to thin. Below them, light; that wasn't harsh, or blinding, but warm and rising.

The engines hummed.

The plane began to descend.

Into something that was no longer sky.

Into peace.

Into light.

David Teahan

# The Letter in the Forest

*If anyone finds this please, I beg you, don't look for us.*

My name is Claire Hargrove. We came into the forest three days ago my husband Mark, our daughter Lily, and I. It was meant to be a reset. One last try to fix the frayed edges that had started to split between my husband and I. We'd rented a cabin off the main trail through a listing in the back pages of a camping newsletter we had subscribed to; something rustic, quiet, disconnected.

I remember the moment we stepped out of the car. The silence was immediate... Just... existing. As if the forest had lungs and held its breath when we entered.

I didn't say anything. I told myself I was tired. It was just the car journey had been long, and the weight of work and everything we hadn't said had taken its toll on both of us.

Lily had heard more than she should have. She'd heard the late-night arguments, the sharp whispers behind closed doors, the silence that followed too many dinners. We thought we were being subtle. We weren't. She heard it all; more than we'd realised.

The cabin was farther in than we expected. The map said half a kilometre from the parking spot, but it took nearly an hour. The trail seemed to pull and stretch, winding in directions that weren't on the map we had printed. But we made it. We laughed about it then. We stopped laughing the next morning.

That first night, though it was almost perfect. We set up a fire behind the cabin, lit the lanterns we'd packed. We ate pre made pasta and lemon cookies from the supermarket, the kind Lily always picked. We played an old family favourite card game by lantern light and joked about how bad Mark was at remembering the rules. For a few hours, the three of us felt normal. No arguments. No tension. Just the sound of the fire crackling and Lily's laugh echoing into the trees. Like a family should feel.

Lily woke me up before sunrise. She said there was a man outside.

I got up immediately and looked out the window. By the time I looked, no one was there.

Only then did I sit beside her and ask her to describe what she saw. She said the man stood there not doing anything; just standing where the trees thinned near the ridge. Watching the cabin. She said he waved except his hand was clenched in a fist, and only his wrist moved, in slow, unsettling circles.

It was described like someone practising the idea of waving and getting it all wrong.

She said he wore jeans and a red flannel shirt; clothes that could've come from any hardware store, any town nearby. But the way he stood in them made it all feel off to Lily, like a mannequin dressed in someone else's attire. Too still. Too clean. Wasn't right.

I wanted to believe she'd dreamt it. Children make things up. Then again, she was ten. Young enough to be imaginative, but old enough to know the difference between dreams and windows. I tried to shrug it off. But as the day moved on, she grew pale. I watched her fall quiet; her usual chatter gone. It was as if the weight of what she'd seen settled in more heavily with each passing hour; like the memory had planted something in her that was still growing.

Lily kept glancing at the tree line. Once or twice, I caught her squinting like she was trying to see if someone was still there. Every time I asked her what she saw, she changed the subject, eyes darting, lips pressed tight.

Like talking about it might make it come closer.

Despite the unease, we were determined to make the most of the break. That first night had been good, almost healing, and I clung to that memory like a lifeline.

Mark helped with that. His presence was always grounding. Broad shouldered and calm, he made me feel like nothing could get past him. I remember watching him chop firewood that first night, his silhouette solid and sure against the flicker of lantern light. I think part of me believed, foolishly, that his strength could keep the forest at bay. That if something came for us, it would have to go through him first.

That night, my husband locked every door and window. I think he was putting on a brave face for us. But I heard Mark pacing, long after he said goodnight.

Back when we first met, it was that same steadiness and his quiet confidence, the sense that he could protect us from anything, that drew me to him. Mark was my lighthouse in the storm. I married him because I believed, deep down, that he would always know what to do when things got dark.

On the morning of our second full day, our phones stopped working. No signal. Not even GPS. As the hours passed, subtle changes began to press in around us.

The trees looked closer to the cabin like they'd crept forward during the night. The grass seemed a little taller. And the light filtering between the branches was wrong: the angles too shallow, the sun shifting backward instead of forward, as if time itself had snagged on something in the canopy.

We tried to console each other. We thought at first maybe it was some sort of mushroom from the forest, or fungi causing some kind of psychotropic effect. Mark laughed it off nervously trying hard to be our rock. I could see it in the way he kept checking the windows, then catching himself and pretending everything was fine.

I, through a trembling voice, reassured Lily everything was going to be okay, even though my hands wouldn't stop shaking.

Towards the front of the cabin, Mark called for me; his voice sharp, uneasy. He stood aghast, pointing. The trail that would lead us back to the car was *gone*, buried under a thick, choking mat of yellow starthistle.

The weed stretched densely between the trees, bristling like it had been growing for years. It was *snarled, tangled*. Like the path had never existed at all.

We stayed near the cabin. But the forest continued to change.

Sounds didn't come from where they should. Birdsong echoed before the birds arrived. A branch would snap beside us, but nothing moved.

At one point, I looked up and saw what I swear was our car, parked between two trees. But when I blinked, it was just brush and bark.

Terrified and directionless, I discussed the situation hoping that my rock Mark would have some guidance, some hope. But I could see he was equally terrified.

We considered walking; just heading in any direction and hoping for the best but the forest no longer felt navigable. The trees shifted subtly. The light changed depending on where you stood. And the yellow starthistle now stretched endlessly in every direction like a barricade. Mark resolved that we should stay put, reasoning that at least the cabin offered food and warmth. One of his last attempts at reassurance was mentioning that, at the very least, nothing had changed inside the cabin…

That night, we heard the *whispering*. The whispering, as if 'the' horror had found its breath.

It wasn't loud at all. Just under the window. Like breath trying to be words. We moved rooms, pressing deeper into the cabin, as if walls could protect us. But the whispering followed, slipping through wood and silence. We still heard it. I wanted to leave. My husband said we should wait till morning. Try again when it's light, he said.

That night Lily took hours to go to sleep. She just stared at the ceiling, her mouth moving silently. I held her close, whispering reassurances I no longer believed. I could feel her trembling under my arms, and though I wanted to be strong for her, part of me wished someone would hold me the same way.

In the morning, the cabin was *different*. It had two windows on the left side yesterday. Now it had one. The door faced a different direction.

Lily was gone.

We didn't hear her leave. We searched every inch of the forest around us for hours, but always within view of the cabin.

I wish I could say we ran deeper, without caution or thought, but the truth is fear anchored us.

Despite Lily being our only child, the forest had made itself something larger than grief. Something older. The fear was heavier than the hope.

Mark ran in frantic loops, calling her name until his voice fractured. He collapsed near the tree line, hoarse and wild eyed.

He stayed there for what felt like hours, curled on the edge of the woods, whimpering like a maimed animal. He didn't speak.

I waited inside the cabin, rocking quietly in the corner. Too afraid to call out.

When he came back, he was... *wrong*. He looked like himself, but something about his face was unfamiliar. His eyes didn't meet mine. His voice didn't carry the same weight.

He asked me to come with him. Mark said he had found the trail.

I said no. He stood at the doorway for a long time. Then he smiled. It was wide and empty. All of that grief in his face was gone, replaced with an emotionless blank canvas, like someone had wiped clean the part of him that once knew what it meant to hurt.

He turned and walked into the trees.

After that, I broke. The tears came in waves I couldn't stop, and I slipped into something close to a catatonic state and curled up for what might have been days. I don't remember sleeping. I don't remember eating. I just rocked in place, whispering their names like prayers that wouldn't rise. I was a mother, a wife. And there was no one left to be either for.

I haven't seen either of them since.

But I hear them. At night. Sometimes during the day. Lily's voice is closer now. But she says things she never would have said.

I found my journal this afternoon, tucked into a part of the cabin I don't remember existing. I don't know if I wrote this for myself, or for you.

But if you're reading it. *Leave*. Leave now.

There's something here. It wears the forest like skin.

It waits for families.

It waits for people who want to start over.

Don't follow our footprints. They go in circles.

Don't follow our voices. They aren't ours.

If you see the cabin, turn around.

If you see a child waving? Don't wave back.

*C.H.*

# The Hum

Harold Whitman had always loved the quiet.

Retired now, after 38 years at a bank where the ticking of the wall clock had served as a metronome to his career, he had traded ledgers and lunch breaks for a small house on the edge of town. No wife. No kids. Just peace. The days passed gently in routine; coffee at seven, the paper by eight, a slow walk through the garden, maybe a documentary in the afternoon. At night, Harold would read, and then sleep deeply, wrapped in silence.

Sometimes he thought about the life that might have been. The girl from the filing room; the one with the green earrings and a laugh that was unrestrained, blissful and full of energy; energy that Harold lacked in his own life.

He had meant to ask her to lunch once; instead, time passed, she became married, his hope being replaced with awkward strained smiles when he passed her in the hallway. That was thirty years ago. There'd been talk of travel in his twenties, or teaching, or music, even. But banking had been safe. Reliable. Now, the silence at night reminded him of how little sound he had made in the world.

Until the hum.

It started on a Tuesday. A faint, low vibration.

Maybe it wasn't even a noise, really; more a presence? Like the sound a refrigerator makes, except there was no fridge nearby. He sat up in bed and listened. It was distant. Barely there.

He dismissed it.

But the next night, it returned. Slightly louder. Still soft, still far off, but enough to keep him awake.

David Teahan

By the fourth night, Harold had placed a pillow over his head. The hum had become a presence in the room. Persistent. Constant. Always humming at the edge of perception.

He bought earbuds. They didn't work. He tried a white noise machine; the hum cut through it like it wasn't even there. He tried soft music, then loud music. Still there.

On Sunday, he asked his friend Gerald, the only person who still visited, mostly out of pity, if he could hear it.

"Hear what?" Gerald had said, sipping tea, eyes flicking to his watch, already rehearsing a polite excuse to leave.

"The hum. It's... it's there every night."

Gerald shook his head. "Maybe it's tinnitus. That happens, you know. At our age."

But Harold didn't think it was in his ears. It felt like it was in the walls. In the air. In the house itself. Gerald left quickly after that, muttering something vague about needing to check on his car.

As time wore on Harold was growing increasingly frantic.

By the following week, he had begun sealing the windows. Hammering thick cork board and plywood over them. Lining the walls with blankets. Anything to trap the hum outside. But in time he realised it wasn't outside.

He knew it now.

It was closer.

It was inside.

But inside what? The house? It came with him, wherever he went. His not-so-silent passenger in this journey of retired isolation. Always there. Pressing on him. An invisible force.

He stormed through hardware stores, muttering about soundproofing foam and acoustic insulation. He padded the bedroom, covered vents, stuffed towels under every door. He stayed up until dawn with a hammer in one hand and his heart in the other.

One morning, he found himself writing notes to himself on sticky pads. "THE HUM ISN'T REAL." "DO NOT TRUST THEM." "KEEP MOVING."

He tried sleeping in the basement. In the shed. In his car. The hum followed, steady as a heartbeat. Louder now.

One night, in desperation, he unplugged every appliance. Flipped the breaker. Lit candles instead of using lights. Curled into a corner of the room hoping somehow the 90-degree angles of the wall could protect him from what was within.

Still, it hummed.

The only time it faded was when he was moving; walking, cleaning, even muttering to himself. But the moment he stopped, it crept back in.

He started talking to himself just to drown it out. Short phrases. Then long monologues. Then arguments. Screaming matches with the silence that wasn't silent.

He stopped answering the phone.

He stopped bathing.

Gerald stopped coming by.

David Teahan

And then, one night, something changed.

He woke up not with the hum in his ears, but in his bones. It didn't sound like a machine any more. It sounded like a choir, low and slow and full of meaning he couldn't translate. It resonated in his chest like music. Like truth.

He lay still for hours, vibrating with it.

And then it spoke.

In what could be described as a knowing. A whisper beneath the tone:

"You are almost ready."

Harold cried, but the emotion within him was not fear or sadness.

It was a cry of relief.

The next night, neighbours noticed his bedroom light stayed on well past midnight. Some said they saw him standing perfectly still in the window at dawn, arms at his side, eyes wide open.

A few mentioned in kitchen conversations quietly, that they thought they heard something. A low vibration in the air.

The next morning, he looked rested. Healthier than he had in weeks. A soft smile played on his lips. The hum no longer bothered him.

Because now, it filled him.

He moved with calm, with poise. He made tea. Washed the dishes. Sat quietly in his chair and listened. Sometimes, he would tap the table in odd rhythms, patterns that didn't quite match anything, unless you were listening closely.

And there, in the vibration that once drove him to madness, he found something unexpected:

Fulfilment.

A sense of completion. A purpose.

All those decades in the bank, all those missed chances and faded friendships they no longer mattered. None of it did.

The hum had come.

And in its frequency, he had become whole.

He closed his eyes, and smiled.

The house was silent, but far from empty.

*The silence hummed.*

# The Form

Daniel first noticed the envelope because it didn't have his name. No address either; just a seal, embossed in dull grey:

**Office of Unrecognised Actions.**

He turned it over in his hands twice. The paper felt strange. It wasn't plastic or that slightly stiff recycled paper. It had a faintly abrasive quality, like something meant to leave a trace on the fingertips. As if it had been manufactured just for this moment. Unnervingly deliberate, rough in a way that felt like it was meant to linger in its texture.

Inside: a single sheet.

*Dear Daniel,*

*Our records indicate a failure to submit Form 908-B regarding an unrecognised action occurring Thursday 15th of August at 14:45. This omission may lead to compliance penalties if not addressed within five working days.*

*Please note: your action does not align with the new behavioural standards established by the Executive Branch. This incident has been recorded.*

*Your cooperation is appreciated.*

Daniel checked the date. Last Thursday? He thought back. He remembered making coffee, reading the news online. Watching a pigeon land on the windowsill. Filling out a web form to unsubscribe from an email list. Watching YouTube videos.

Nothing illegal. Nothing… worth recognising.

The envelope had no return address. Just the seal again, in miniature.

He set it aside.

---

By Monday, a second letter had arrived. Identical. Except this one had a small, red stamp in the corner:

*First Notice.*

That evening, he googled Office of Unrecognised Actions.

Nothing official. Nothing but a forgotten Reddit thread from 2021. Someone had posted a blurry scan of a similar letter. Three replies, each one the usual Reddit fare: a joke about conspiracy theories, a snide remark about bureaucracy, and someone asking if it was just a viral marketing stunt.

He tried the phone number on the letter. After a long pause it rang six times, then a recorded voice spoke:

*Your query has been logged. Do not attempt further clarification.*

The phone was filled with a piercing sound Something between a modem dial tone and an air raid siren. Then the line disconnected, as if in protest to having been dialled at all.

---

By Friday, a third envelope arrived. Red ink this time.

This one included a QR code in the bottom corner. Black on grey, etched into the paper as if it had always been there, waiting to be scanned.

*This is your Final Warning.*

*Continued failure to submit Form 908-B will result in escalated intervention.*

Later that day on his walk, Daniel noticed someone had painted *908-B?* on the sidewalk outside his building in bright red spray. It appeared stencilled; precise and official-looking, unlike the erratic tags he was used to downtown. It felt more like a warning than graffiti.

Of course it was directed at Daniel. There was no such thing as coincidence anymore not when the warnings were stencilled in red, precise and surgically timed.

Daniel didn't need to know. The system didn't make mistakes; it only made decisions.

On his return, Miriam from upstairs entered the elevator. They had known each other for years and shared a quiet camaraderie over broken heating, bad coffee, and the weather. But today, she said nothing. When he greeted her, she kept her eyes fixed on the floor, arms rigid at her sides. She didn't strike him as distracted or annoyed. Rather, afraid. Afraid to make eye contact, as if acknowledgment itself might be flagged.

He cracked on Saturday. The pressure had been mounting. The sensation building. Subtle, pervasive.

It had been three letters now. Three letters, a curb side warning, and a series of increasingly awkward interactions: eyes averted, greetings withheld, moments where recognition seemed to falter and correct itself mid breath. Even the barista at his local café seemed to hesitate before asking his name.

He gave in and scanned the QR code from the letter, opening the form on his phone.

It opened in a secure browser window. The header read:

> *Office of Unrecognised Actions*
>
> *Behavioural Audit Division.*

The font was a bright red, glaringly so. An almost punishing hue that felt like it was chosen to discourage reading. It made his eyes ache.

Thirty-nine questions.

The first page was easy: Name, address, ID number. All optional.

Then:

> *Describe the action you believe may have occurred at the stated time.*
>
> *Made tea. Seen a bird. Watched YouTube.*
>
> *Who, if anyone, witnessed or influenced this action?*

[blank]

> *Have you recently experienced the sensation of being misremembered, overlooked, or partially erased from others' awareness?*

Yes.

> *How did the action make you feel?*

Normal at the time, but later it hurt. Hurt in a quiet way, the kind that comes from being unseen by people who once knew your name, your routine, your presence. He didn't know the action was unrecognised, but he felt the sting of being forgotten.

*Are you certain it occurred?*

Daniel stared at the blinking cursor, rubbing his eyes. Less tired and more from the quiet sting of doubt.

He submitted the form.

---

No letters came the following week. The silence felt sterile, like a system that had moved him from one column to another. A bureaucratic shrug in digital form.

Maybe he would find peace. Maybe the bureaucracy had forgotten about him.

The thought was oddly comforting, like being misplaced in a filing cabinet no one opened anymore. He tried to laugh it off thinking of all the stories he'd heard over the years about endless queues, missing paperwork, departments that lost their own phone numbers. It had always been a joke.

Until it wasn't.

The pharmacist, who once greeted him with easy familiarity, now offered only a clinical smile. "New customer?" she asked, her tone flat. Daniel protested, he'd been coming there for years. But she typed his name like it was unfamiliar, a typo to be corrected. His depression medication was no longer on record. Vanished without explanation.

It stung more than it should have, this quiet unseeing by people who once waved.

At work, his security badge needed reactivation. "Says you've been away longer than a week," the receptionist said. "Were you on leave?"

He hadn't been.

---

Three weeks later, a new envelope arrived. It was thinner this time, as if the paper itself had been engineered for discretion.

The kind used when a system wanted to say something without being seen saying it. It felt cheaper, colder. Designed for mass issuance.

> *Your Form 908-B was accepted. However, inconsistencies in your behavioural pattern suggest recent deviations. Please complete Addendum 12-C in accordance with Article 7 of the Behavioural Standards Framework.*

He scanned another QR code. It had been printed faintly along the inside fold of the new envelope.

It was shorter. Just nine questions:

> *Have you lied to yourself in the past 10 days?*
>
> *Have others behaved as if your absence was expected?*
>
> *Do you still consider yourself Daniel?*

He answered honestly. At least, he thought he did.

Submitted.

---

Things grew quieter. Or maybe he did. Silence had become a kind of uniform, blending him into the softened static of official toleration.

The sidewalk remained clean, unnaturally so. As if someone had meticulously scrubbed away the previous marks, stripping a layer of concrete in the process.

It wasn't just sanitation; it was erasure.

The neighbours no longer said hello. Their doors closed more quickly when he passed, and conversations dulled or stopped mid-sentence. Daniel noticed. It hurt more than he expected; this slow, polite disappearing by people who once smiled in passing.

Daniel had always been quiet. Introverted. Before the letters, that simply meant he preferred calm over chaos. He liked silent cafés, solo walks, and the kind of friendships that didn't need daily maintenance. He'd once spent an entire weekend reorganising his bookshelf by theme; delighted, rather than lonely. But now, that same quietness seemed to work against him.

He was the kind of man who gave others space in elevators and avoided confrontation at all costs. He didn't raise his voice or challenge what was happening around him. He internalised, processed, nodded.

He told himself it was easier that way.

At the grocery store, his usual checkout line was closed. Always unusually quiet. Self-checkout failed to scan his items. A young clerk waved him to a kiosk with a manual override. She didn't smile. She didn't even nod. Her hand hovered near the override key like it was a security trigger, rather than a button.

Daniel began receiving notices again. These new ones were not warnings, but observations. Soft flags from the system, like the polite cough of someone about to correct your posture at a formal dinner.

*We've detected minor inconsistencies in your recent purchases.*

*You appear to have deviated from typical walking routes.*

*A recent expression you made was flagged as contextually ambiguous.*

Each came with a new form, as mandated under the Executive Oversight Protocol. Shorter. Stranger.

One asked him to rank his emotional opacity on a scale of 1 to 12.

Another offered a list of statements and asked him to delete the one that didn't hurt.

---

He still went to work. Still paid rent. Still drank coffee. Still existed within the boundaries of the Acceptable Behaviour Matrix.

But he rarely looked people in the eye. It felt like eye contact had become a signal; one he no longer understood, and no longer trusted. As if the mere act of engaging would somehow flag to the system another discrepancy.

He found it easier not to notice when someone passed by and seemed surprised to see him. As if *he* was the one disturbing *them*.

With his quiet posture, his lowered eyes, his hesitant smile, he made it easy for others to pretend he didn't belong. Easy to frame the discomfort as his fault. As if his meekness invited erasure.

Sometimes, he wondered what would happen if he ever stopped submitting forms. Just... stopped. Quietly. Without explanation. Would the system even notice? Or would it pause for a moment, puzzled, before replacing him with someone easier to calibrate?

Or if submitting was now just something he did, automatically: like breathing, or blinking, or not speaking when he didn't have the right words.

---

In the end, Daniel wasn't punished.

He was, by all accounts, fully compliant. Not out of loyalty or belief, but because every letter, every form, every silent social correction had gradually reshaped him.

His compliance wasn't chosen; it was coaxed, layered into his habits until resistance became unthinkable.

Recognised.

Predictable.

Quiet.

# The Cultures That Spoke Back

Dr. Malcolm Reeves didn't believe in anything he couldn't measure.

Over twenty years in microbiology had stripped him of all but the most rational instincts. He trusted patterns, probabilities, the sterile quiet of labs, and the language of data. And it was in that silence, late on a Thursday evening, that the unease began.

The lab at Ashridge University was empty, save for the soft hum of cooling units and the rhythmic tick of the digital incubator. Malcolm was reviewing growth rates from a new set of samples recovered from a remote, sealed cave system in the Denisova region of Siberia. Organisms isolated for tens of thousands of years. Extremophiles. Hardy and strange, qualities that stood in quiet defiance of everything Malcolm was. He was precise, conflict averse, the kind of man who apologised when others bumped into him. Even the lab coat seemed to hang shyly on his frame.

Denisova Cave is the only known site where remains of the Denisovans have been found; an archaic human species whose genetics still linger in parts of modern humanity. The thought crossed Malcolm's mind once, in passing, before he dismissed it. He preferred not to speculate. He was not paid to speculate. But somewhere, buried beneath layers of professional detachment, he felt the cave had waited a long time to be opened.

He leaned over a Petri dish labelled Sample D-7. The bacteria inside were oddly cooperative, arranging themselves into symmetrical lines. He adjusted the microscope and frowned. The formation was too ordered. It wasn't like colonies expanding toward nutrients. More like... glyphs.

He rubbed his temples and typed a note.

D-7 forming repeating structures not unlike runes. Possibly contamination or anomalous cohesion behaviour.

He introduced a minor stressor. A change in salinity, and waited. The glyphs shifted. Not randomly, or dissolving, but as if recalibrating. Malcolm sat back, watching as the structures realigned into tighter symmetry.

The overhead lights flickered once. Then again.

He glanced at the lab's environmental monitor. A spike. Brief. Unusual.

"Static discharge," he muttered, though his voice lacked confidence.

Before leaving, he printed a high-resolution photo of the dish. He slipped it into his notebook to review at home.

The shapes intrigued him.

At home, the photo sat on his desk under the glow of a tungsten lamp. Malcolm sipped black tea. It was plain, comfortless, and as unadorned as his personality; eyes flicking between the print and his laptop, running image pattern software. The results were inconclusive, but the symmetry, the fractal-like branching, it didn't match known bacterial behaviour.

Behind him, the radio crackled. Then hissed. Then played static.

He turned, puzzled. The radio was off.

He checked. The dial had moved to an unused frequency.

He turned it off again, firmly this time.

Ten minutes later, the printer behind him whirred to life.

He jumped.

It spat out another copy of the photo. But the glyphs were different. Subtly. Shifted. Narrower. Angled like a different dialect of the same language.

He checked the timestamp on the printer log. It read: 3:14 a.m.

*Odd.* It was barely 10:30 p.m.

That night, he dreamed he was back in the lab. The dish pulsed with a soft blue light. He leaned close. And something in the Petri dish looked back.

Malcolm awoke with a start. Darkness still blanketed the house. He blinked, sat up, and noticed a faint glow seeping from under his study door.

He opened it slowly.

The original printed photo glowed faintly on the desk. *Phosphorescent. Impossible.*

Condensation fogged the window from the chill night air outside, coating the glass like breath held too long. As he approached, he saw marks forming in the moisture. Glyphs. The same as the dish.

His reflection in the glass flickered; for a moment, the face looking back wasn't his. The brow was heavier, the cheekbones broader, the eyes deep set and ancient; bearing the rugged symmetry of something half remembered from anthropology texts. A Neanderthal echo, staring out from beneath his skin.

He stumbled back, knocking over the chair. The whispers began again. Soft. Almost polite.

"Malcolm."

David Teahan

114

He clutched the desk. Eyes wide. Breath shallow.

The Petri dish was in the lab. This was a printout. This shouldn't be happening.

By morning, Malcolm's face was pale, drawn. He had spent most of the night awake in bed, gripping his blanket like a child and staring at the ceiling in disbelief. There was a distant look in his eyes now, as though part of him had stayed behind in the shadows of the night. He returned to the lab, clutching his notebook tightly, as if it could anchor him to what little reality he still believed in.

The culture had overgrown its boundaries, spreading across the glass and underneath the dish lid. He moved to incinerate it but the steriliser failed. Power error. He checked the breaker. All systems normal.

His monitor lit up with lines of text. It wasn't English, or computer code. The glyphs.

Then, they faded, and in plain font: STAY

He backed away.

The assistant, a young woman named Lena, arrived to find him seated before the incubator, unmoving. She paused in the doorway, an expression of confusion. Something about his face looked... different. More angular. More ancient.

"Dr. Reeves? Are you alright?"

He did not answer.

His lips moved, barely.

Whispers. No sound.

Lena lingered for a moment longer, concern etched into her expression, then turned and walked quickly away down the corridor. She didn't want to disturb the professor; it didn't feel like her place. Hierarchy demanded distance, even when instinct whispered otherwise.

The culture was now growing in dishes he hadn't touched. Glyphs appearing like clockwork. The room itself began to shimmer faintly at the edges, as if the patterns were no longer confined to glass and ink, but radiating outward. They were etching themselves invisibly onto air, tile, and reality itself.

Malcolm came in daily, never speaking, only writing.

Glyph after glyph. Some now bore a resemblance. Unmistakably reminiscent of ancient symbolic motifs, like those found on artifacts unearthed near Denisova Cave. He hadn't thought of the cave in days, yet now its shadow returned, threading through the shapes on the page.

The patterns grew more elaborate. Symmetry gave way to depth. Dimension.

Malcolm's behaviour grew increasingly erratic. He spoke to no one, often staring at blank surfaces for minutes on end as if waiting for something to appear. He would pause mid step in the hallway; eyes locked on some unseen geometry only he seemed to understand. His notes became unreadable to others filled with shapes instead of words.

Strangest of all, no one else saw the glyphs. Not Lena. Not the technicians. The Petri dishes appeared ordinary to them, the patterns nonsensical or absent altogether. Only Malcolm seemed able to perceive their shifting order, their impossible language. That Lena left suddenly, without saying goodbye.

In time, Malcolm's notebook filled with symbols no one could decipher.

They weren't discovered. They were waiting.

And he, ever the quiet man, simply listened; first with fear, then with reverence.

Each day, the boundary between observer and subject thinned. The glyphs no longer responded to him; they anticipated him, forming arcs and spirals that aligned with thoughts he had not yet formed. At times, he felt like a conduit, rather than a scientist.

One morning, his writing hand trembled with reverence. The message he inscribed flowed through him, fluent and unbroken, as if dictated by a voice just beyond hearing.

There was no final realisation, no grand epiphany. Only the stillness of a man who had ceased to ask why.

And in that stillness, something else began.

*"The universe is not only stranger than we suppose, it is stranger than we can suppose."* J.B.S. Haldane

# Pencil Mark

Norman moved through the world like a pencil mark left by a ruler. Straight, faint, and easy to erase.

People passed him without seeing. Not because he was invisible, but because their eyes had been taught what to value, and Norman wasn't on the list. He was short. Worn. His features assembled in a way that unsettled the subconscious; misaligned rather than malformed. As if someone had rushed the job. His nose was a little too big. His forehead seemed to loom a little over the rest of his face. Deep, permanent bags hung under his eyes like echoes of forgotten sleep. No one would ever call his face pleasant. In another era, Norman might have been relegated to sideshows or whispered about in train carriages; his appearance mistaken for spectacle instead of circumstance.

He didn't expect attention. His life was better without that. But sometimes, in the quiet minutes between bus rides or in the dusty light of early morning, he imagined a life with different scaffolding. One where he'd been taught how to speak with ease, where he hadn't been left in the care of flickering televisions and cupboards filled with canned food.

Norman read, though. He read everything. Instruction manuals, library books, those free newspapers people left crumpled on benches. He remembered facts with uncanny clarity. Dates, formulas, old city names. If you gave him a moment, he could tell you the boiling point of antifreeze or the migratory pattern of monarch butterflies.

But no one asked.

He was thirty-five, though most wouldn't have guessed. It wasn't because he looked older, but because he looked like someone time had never properly claimed. An unusual combination of short stature and weathered, craggy features made Norman difficult to place; like a face seen in a half-remembered dream or old photograph, without quite fitting the time or place around it.

At 4:03 PM, like most weekdays, Norman left work exactly on time. He wore factory floor overalls: navy blue, stained at the knees and along the cuffs with permanent grease marks from years of unnoticed labour. His hands, though washed, still carried the scent of machine oil.

He'd worked at the same auto parts workshop since finishing school. He wasn't a mechanic or assembler as those roles required certifications and confidence, but as a floater. He swept the concrete floors. He checked the soap dispensers. He refilled the old oil drums with trembling precision, double checking the volume even though no one else did. He was dependable, quiet, and forgettable.

No one disliked Norman. But no one remembered his birthday either.

The bus ride home took seventeen minutes. He always sat by the window to avoid being looked at. The same houses blurred past in rusted reds and weary greys, the same overgrown footpaths, the same tired signage half flapping in the wind. A discount pharmacy. A laundromat that hadn't changed its prices in five years. A church sign with letters missing.

When his stop arrived, Norman stepped off with the same rhythm he always had with one hand on the rail, one eye on the ground.

He didn't go straight home.

Two blocks east was the corner shop. It wasn't remarkable: a narrow store front with hand drawn chalkboard signs and dusty windows covered by old posters. The woman who worked there had a habit of looking everyone in the eye when she spoke. It was, perhaps, the kindest thing Norman had known in years.

He walked past it slowly. He didn't go in.

Instead, he carried on with the footpath tilting slightly beneath his steps as if the ground itself weren't sure of him. A dog barked from behind a fence. Somewhere, a sprinkler ticked in lazy rotation.

Norman adjusted the strap of his bag and walked home.

Once home, Norman repeated his nightly routine with quiet precision. He showered, placed a frozen dinner in the microwave, and fed his goldfish, Stevey. Then he turned on his computer to play a single player strategy game that gave him the comforting illusion of control; territories to defend, choices that mattered.

After a few hours, he would retire to bed and set his two alarms for the next morning; one to wake him, one just in case. There was a rhythm to it all. A structure. A framework he could live within. He was quietly proud of that.

He never drank alcohol. Once, in his teens, he had tried weed behind the school oval. But after a childhood shaped by the chaos of drug-addicted parents, Norman had developed a deep and permanent fear of losing control.

He couldn't recall the last time he had seen them. He didn't want to. He didn't miss them. In truth, he still doubted they noticed when he left home at sixteen. Or if his father just turned up the volume on the tv and opened another beer.

The next morning, Norman spoke to Stevey while pulling on his work socks.

"Think today's the day, Stevey?" he asked, staring into the tank.

Stevey hovered near the filter intake, bumping lightly against the current caused by the filter.

"Maybe I'll try again. Just say something simple. Nice weather, or the colour of the biscuits she stocks. That wouldn't be weird, right?"

Stevey nibbled at a corner of the decorative shipwreck.

Norman nodded as if Stevey had confirmed it. "Right. Keep it simple. Normal."

Stevey swam a lazy loop and returned to his post by the glass.

Norman checked his reflection in the microwave door, ran a wet hand over his hair, and gave Stevey a final look. "You've got the easy life, mate. Just float and forget."

The goldfish blinked, slow and blank-eyed, as Norman grabbed his bag and stepped out the door.

Halfway through the workday, Norman sat down in the lunch room with a reheated sausage roll and a thermos of tea. The mechanics used the occasion to gently rib him.

"Norman, when you gonna get married, mate? What about Martha? She's three times the size of you, but reckon you could handle her!" one laughed, referring to the office secretary with a grin and a wink.

Norman chuckled softly. It was easier to go along with their brand of humour than resist it. A few years ago, they'd laughed about the hair at the nape of his neck and how it trailed down into his shirt like a pelt. They used to call him Ape Man, a joke that lasted a whole year.

Eventually, Norman had bleached it with peroxide in secret, hoping to stop the growth. It had worked, in a way. The hair never came back only the scarring did. But at least they didn't laugh any more.

That afternoon, the shop was still open when Norman passed. The chalkboard out front advertised hazelnut biscuits and chamomile tea. He didn't hesitate this time.

The bell above the door gave a quiet chime as he entered. The woman behind the counter glanced up and smiled with a real, reflexive softness. Her smile lived in her cheeks and eyes, not just her mouth.

She was beautiful. It couldn't be said in a movie star way, but in a way that was real, that no Instagram filter could properly capture; warm skin, slightly messy bun, a freckle near the edge of her lip that drew the eye without trying. She looked like someone who listened closely. Who remembered names. Who maybe grew herbs in little pots near the window.

"Afternoon," she said, with a radiant smile, as if greeting an old friend rather than a man she'd likely forgotten came in at all.

Norman nodded, shy but steady. "Just looking, thanks."

She nodded and returned to tidying the counter. The air smelt like cinnamon and soap.

He lingered for a minute. Looked at the biscuit tins. Picked up a jar of jam he didn't need. His heart thudded behind his ribs in a quiet, persistent rhythm.

Then he placed the jar back and nodded again. "Thanks. See you."

"Have a good one," she said, her voice full of ease.

Norman stepped back into the street and exhaled.

That night, he spoke to Stevey again.

"Well... I went in," he said, lowering himself into the chair beside the tank.

Stevey was circling the rim of the fake coral cave, slow and oblivious.

"Didn't say much. Just looked around like usual. Picked up a jar and put it back down."

Stevey paused, then drifted lazily through a strand of green plastic kelp.

"She smiled. Not at the jar, obviously. At me. Same as always. But it felt warmer today. Or maybe that's just me wanting it to."

Stevey blinked and bumped against the glass with a soft tap.

Norman leaned back and looked up at the ceiling. "Anyway... just wanted you to know I didn't chicken out. Not completely."

He fed Stevey a single pinch of flakes. The goldfish surfaced quickly, mouth gaping with instinct.

Norman watched until the tank settled, the water quiet again.

Then he turned off the light and made his way to bed, the hum of the filter soft as the room settling. Sleep came quickly, with the memory of her soft eyes and smile lingering like warmth from a hand that had barely brushed his.

The next afternoon, Norman walked into the shop again.

He'd practised a line in his head: something light about the weather or the biscuits. Something normal.

The woman was restocking tea boxes behind the counter. She greeted him with her usual smile.

"Back again," she said cheerfully.

Norman felt his throat tighten, but the line came out: "Yeah. I thought I'd try those hazelnut ones today. You said they're good, right?"

She paused. Her smile faltered just slightly, a fraction too long. It was a subtle change. The kind that arrived without alarms, but with the quiet retraction of warmth. Norman had seen it many times in his life. A smile that didn't reach the eyes. A slight lean away. The way people pulled politeness around themselves like a coat in sudden cold. Then she nodded. "Sure. They're on the second shelf."

Norman found the biscuits. Brought them to the counter. Her hands moved quickly through the register routine.

"Anything else?" she asked.

"No, that's all. Just... thank you."

He tried to hold her gaze as he said it.

She didn't meet it this time. Just handed him the bag and said, "Have a good one." Norman, eyes still focused on her, remembered back to his conversation with Stevey. He was determined for it to work this time. He had to try.

With no eye contact between them, Norman stammered, "Oh umm. I was just... I just thought…"

Beads of sweat began to form along his forehead. Anxiety gripped him hard, freezing him in place. He stood there, speechless, flushed, holding a small paper bag in his right hand.

She had stepped back from the counter with a slow, careful retreat, as though he were something unpredictable. As if some wild animal had wandered in, polite but wrong.

Norman didn't understand. Why was she recoiling? Why couldn't he move? His expression shifted into puzzled stillness.

He turned. Quietly. Hurriedly. And stepped out into the street, wiping his forehead with the sleeve of his jumper as he disappeared down the path.

Two days later, he noticed the change.

A new sign on the counter: *Please do not linger in the store unless making a purchase.*

The woman didn't look up when he entered. A man stood behind the counter that day.

Norman bought nothing. He left quietly.

The following morning, he received a message on his phone from the store's generic number:

"Dear customer, please refrain from extended visits that may make staff uncomfortable. We appreciate your understanding."

That night, Norman didn't speak to Stevey. He fed him silently, watched him circle the tank, then turned away.

He sat at his desk with a blank sheet of paper and a pen he hadn't used in months. No salutation. No date. Just the words that came out.

"I wasn't trying to frighten you."

Then, slowly, the rest followed.

"I don't know how people talk. Not really. I try, but it always feels like wearing clothes that don't fit. You were kind to me. Not in a big way. Just enough that it mattered. Enough that I looked forward to Tuesday afternoons more than anything else in my life. That probably sounds sad. Maybe it is. But I'm not broken. Just quiet. And tired. And trying.

You reminded me what kindness looks like. Even if it was just part of your job."

He folded the page. Just once, in half. Then he placed it in the back of the drawer beneath old receipts and a spare pair of shoelaces.

He didn't reread it.

He didn't sign it.

He just sat for a while, hands in his lap, listening to the faint, rhythmic swirl of Stevey's tank.

He never went back to the store. Not that week whole week. Nor ever. Whatever had formed in his mind however faint and hopeful had folded just as easily as the letter now tucked away.

A few days later, while waiting at the bus stop, Norman noticed a butterfly land on his hand. It was pale blue, its wings paper thin, pulsing with each breath of wind.

He didn't move. Just watched it.

No one else seemed to notice. But Norman did.

He watched until it lifted and disappeared into the air; a small, weightless thing going somewhere unseen.

Then he boarded the bus, and went on with his day.

# Afterword

If these stories stirred something in you: a memory, a question, a feeling that lingered, I'd be honoured if you'd consider leaving a review.

Your words help others discover the quiet spaces between the lines.

Thank you for reading.

*David Teahan, Farbellum Publishing*

www.ingramcontent.com/pod-product-compliance
Lightning Source LLC
Chambersburg PA
CBHW072030170626
46811CB00008B/3021